黑暗之心

Heart of Darkness

原著 _ Joseph Conrad
改寫 _ David A. Hill
譯者 _ 林育珊

ABOUT THIS BOOK

For the Student

🎧 Listen to the story and do some activities on your Audio CD.

💬 Talk about the story.

⭐ Prepare for Cambridge English: Preliminary (PET) for schools.

For the Teacher

HELBLING e·ZONE THE EDUCATIONAL PLATFORM   A state-of-the-art interactive learning environment with 1000s of free online self-correcting activities for your chosen readers.

Go to our Readers Resource site for information on using readers and downloadable Resource Sheets, photocopiable Worksheets, and Tapescripts. www.helblingreaders.com

For lots of great ideas on using Graded Readers consult Reading Matters, the Teacher's Guide to using Helbling Readers.

Level 5 Structures

Modal verb **would**	Non-defining relative clauses
I'd love to . . .	Present perfect continuous
Future continuous	Used to / would
Present perfect future	Used to / used to doing
Reported speech / verbs / questions	Second conditional
Past perfect	Expressing wishes and regrets
Defining relative clauses	

Structures from other levels are also included.

CONTENTS

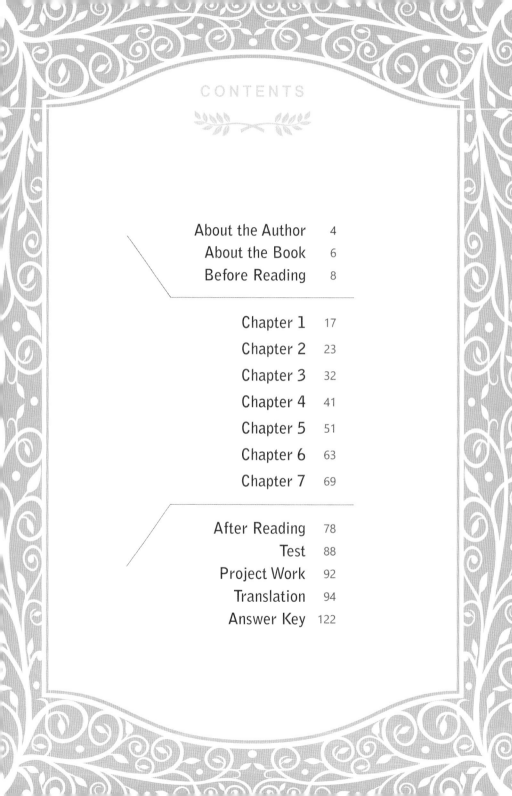

ABOUT THE AUTHOR

Joseph Conrad was born in 1857, in Berdychiv, part of the Polish Ukraine. His real name was Jozef Teodor Konrad Nalecz Korzeniowski. Conrad lived in the Ukraine[1] and Russia as a child and after the death of both of his parents, he was looked after[2] by his uncle in Poland.

From an early age he learnt French, read Shakespeare and became very fond of the Polish[3] romantic poets, but he also had a passion[4] for the sea. His uncle allowed him to go to sea[5] as soon as he had finished school and in 1878, he joined the British Merchant[6] Navy[7], eventually becoming a captain.

Conrad sailed extensively[8] all over the world and in 1890 he went to the Belgian[9] Congo, which was later his inspiration[10] for *Heart of Darkness* (1902). This journey, however, made Conrad ill and in 1894, he gave up[11] the sea to become a full-time writer, mainly because of his health problems.

In 1886 Conrad obtained[12] British nationality[13] and when he left the navy he settled[14] in the south of England. In 1895, his first novel—*Almayer's Folly*, an adventure set on the coast of Borneo[15]—was published. In 1896 he married Jessie George and they had two sons. He regularly published short stories, novels and essays[16], but was not financially[17] successful until 1913, when his novel *Chance* became popular.

Conrad was widely recognized[18] as a remarkable[19] writer by other writers, and his novels *Lord Jim* (1900), *Heart of Darkness* (1902), *Nostromo* (1904), *The Secret Agent* (1907) and *Under Western Eyes* (1911) were highly praised. His ability to handle English with such style is even more impressive when one thinks that it was his third language. Conrad died of[20] a heart attack[21] in 1924.

1 Ukraine [ˈjukren] (n.) 烏克蘭
2 look after 照顧
3 Polish [ˈpolɪʃ] (a.) 波蘭的
4 passion [ˈpæʃən] (n.) 熱情
5 go to sea 去當水手；出海
6 merchant [ˈmɝtʃənt] (a.) 商業的
7 navy [ˈnevɪ] (n.) 海軍；艦隊
8 extensively [ɪkˈstɛnsɪvlɪ] (adv.) 到處
9 Belgian [ˈbɛldʒən] (a.) 比利時的
10 inspiration [ˌɪnspəˈreʃən] (n.) 靈感
11 give up 放棄

12 obtain [əbˈten] (v.) 獲得
13 nationality [ˌnæʃənˈælətɪ] (n.) 國籍
14 settle [ˈsɛtl] (v.) 定居
15 Borneo [ˈbɔrnɪˌo] (n.) 婆羅洲
16 essay [ˈɛse] (n.) 散文
17 financially [faɪˈnænʃəlɪ] (adv.) 財務地
18 recognize [ˈrɛkəgˌnaɪz] (v.) 承認
19 remarkable [rɪˈmɑrkəbl] (a.) 值得注意的；卓越的
20 die of 死於（某疾病）
21 heart attack 心臟病；心臟衰竭

Heart of Darkness, like many of Joseph Conrad's novels, is based on his own experience as a sailor. This story is closely connected to the period that he spent working for a Belgian trading company[1] on a river steamer[2] on the Congo River, which he captained for a short time. He returned sick, and disillusioned[3] with the Belgians' imperialistic[4] attitude[5] to the local people.

There are two narrators[6] in *Heart of Darkness*: an anonymous[7] narrator on board[8] the *Nellie* and Marlow. The first narrator starts the novel and then introduces Marlow, who then in turn[9] tells his story. At the end of Marlow's story, the anonymous narrator then finishes the novel in his own words. This technique[10] is called a frame narrative.

The main story in *Heart of Darkness* is the part narrated by the sailor Marlow. He tells some other sailors of his experience as the captain of a steamboat on a large river in Africa. Marlow's job is to transport[11] ivory, and then to go and bring back the company's best ivory agent—Mr Kurtz—who is believed to be sick.

After a long delay because the boat has to be repaired, they sail up the river. They find Kurtz, who seems to have become a leader for the local people. Eventually, Marlow gets him onto the boat, but Kurtz dies on the way back down the river.

The word "darkness" from the title has different symbolic[12] meanings in the text: the jungle, evil, corruption[13] and exploitation[14]. And it seems that, in the end, Mr Kurtz has picked up the "darkness" rather than taking the "light" to the people.

The novel is an attack on colonialism[15] and imperialism[16], although it has been argued that Conrad dehumanizes[17] the Africans, making them no more than a part of the dark and dangerous jungle.

Heart of Darkness has been translated into many languages and adapted[18] for radio and television. The most famous adaptation is Francis Ford Coppola's film *Apocalypse[19] Now* (1979).

1 trading company 貿易公司
2 steamer [ˈstimɚ] (n.) 汽船
3 disillusion [ˌdɪsɪˈljuʒən] (v.) 理想破滅
4 imperialistic [ɪmˌpɪrɪəˈlɪstɪk] (a.) 帝國主義的
5 attitude [ˈætətjud] (n.) 態度
6 narrator [næˈretɚ] (n.) 講述者
7 anonymous [əˈnɑnəməs] (a.) 匿名的
8 on board 在船上
9 in turn 依次
10 technique [tɛkˈnik] (n.) 技術；技巧
11 transport [trænsˈpɔrt] (v.) 運輸
12 symbolic [sɪmˈbɑlɪk] (a.) 象徵性的
13 corruption [kəˈrʌpʃən] (n.) 墮落；腐敗
14 exploitation [ˌɛksplɔɪˈteʃən] (n.) 剝削
15 colonialism [kəˈlonɪəˌlɪzəm] (n.) 殖民主義
16 imperialism [ɪmˈpɪrɪəˌlɪzəm] (n.) 帝國主義
17 dehumanize [dɪˈhjumənˌaɪz] (v.) 獸化；使喪失人性
18 adapt [əˈdæpt] (v.) 改編
19 apocalypse [əˈpɑkəˌlɪps] (n.) 啟示

1 This story focuses on a journey along the Congo River, also known as the Zaire, in Africa in 1902. Look at the pictures and words and then use them to complete these sentences from the story. Look up any words you don't know in a dictionary.

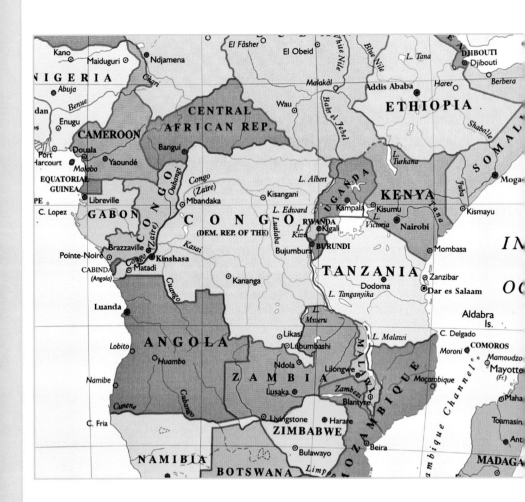

desolate   natives

journey   steamboat

wilderness   canoe

a We followed the coast of Africa which seemed like
the edge of a _____.

b Kurtz's station was empty and _____
in the heart of the jungle.

c The _____' camps surrounded the place,
and the chiefs came to see him every day.

d A lone white man was paddling back in his _____
with four natives.

e But in order to understand the effect this _____
had on me, you need to know a number of things.

f I got a job with the company as the captain of a river
_____.

2 What do you know about the Congo River and the jungle surrounding it? Work with a partner and do some research on the Internet.

3 The main character Marlow says: "I remembered there was a foreign company that traded on the Congo River." Read this definition below.

trade

the action of buying and selling goods and services

In 1902 what goods were taken to Africa and what goods were brought back from Africa by traders? Fill in the lists below, choosing from these items.

BEADS

IVORY

COTTON

ALCOHOL

RUBBER

GOLD

TAKEN TO AFRICA	BROUGHT BACK FROM AFRICA
....	....
....	....
....	....
....	....
....	....

4 Do you know which tragic form of trading once existed in Africa? Do some research on the Internet if necessary.

5 Marlow is the main character and the narrator of the story. Read the description of him and then tick (✓) the best ending to the sentence below.

"Marlow was the only one of us who was still working as a sailor. He was a seaman and a wanderer. He was interested in the ships, the sea, the foreign ports that he visited and the foreign faces that he saw."

_____ Marlow is a typical seaman because _____

    a he is curious and likes adventure.

    b he likes to spend time on his own.

6 Listen to this text about Marlow and his new job and then tick (✓) the correct option.

_____ a Marlow will be working for _____.

    1 a Belgian company

    2 a German company

    3 an English company

_____ ⓑ He will be travelling along the river in a

_____.

① canoe
② cruise ship
③ steamboat

_____ ⓒ How does he feel about this new job?

① worried
② depressed
③ excited

_____ ⓓ On his journey along the Congo River there

will be _____.

① three main stops
② one stop
③ two small stops

7 Listen to the text again and put the names of the stops of Marlow's journey in the correct order. Write 1, 2, 3.

☐ Inner Station
☐ Outer Station
☐ Central Station

8 Kurtz is the other main character in the novel.
He is an ivory agent and a trader.
Read the descriptions of him.
Then match the words with their definitions.

"... a first class agent and a
very remarkable person."

"Kurtz will go very far ...
He will become important in the
administration before long."

"A prodigy ... next year he will
be assistant manager."

1 to be successful

2 extraordinary

3 a talented person

_____ a remarkable

_____ b to go far

_____ c a prodigy

9 What type of job could a man like Kurtz do today? Discuss in class.

10 These are Marlow's thoughts about Kurtz. Complete the sentences with the words below.

imagine
desolate
natives
colleagues
canoe
lone
headquarters
wilderness

"And for the first time I felt I could really ⓐ _____ what Kurtz was like. A ⓑ _____ white man, turning his back on the ⓒ _____ and his ⓓ _____, and paddling back in his ⓔ _____ with four ⓕ _____ , to his empty and ⓖ _____ station in the ⓗ _____."

11 How does Marlow's image of Kurtz differ from the one in Exercise **8**? Discuss with a partner.

Chapter 1

Night was falling. We were sitting on the *Nellie*, a sailing boat. We were anchored[1] in the Thames[2] in London, waiting for the tide to change so that we could leave. The air was dark, and there was a great gloom[3] all over the city. All five of us were experienced sailors and old friends, and we were relaxed together. As the darkness increased, we saw more and more lights on the small boats going backwards and forwards across the river.

"This has also been one of the dark places of the earth," said Marlow suddenly.

Marlow was the only one of us who was still working as a sailor. He was a seaman, and also a wanderer[4]. He was interested in the ships, the sea, the foreign ports[5] that he visited and the foreign faces that he saw. And he was also very interested in understanding deeper and more complex[6] things about the places that he visited and the people that he met. So his remark[7] was not surprising to us, and nobody answered. Then he continued, very slowly:

---

1 anchor [ˈæŋkɚ] (v.) 拋錨泊船
2 Thames [tɛmz] (n.) 泰晤士河
3 gloom [glum] (n.) 陰暗
4 wanderer [ˈwɑndərɚ] (n.) 漫遊者
5 port [port] (n.) 港口
6 complex [ˈkɑmplɛks] (a.) 複雜的
7 remark [rɪˈmɑrk] (n.) 談論

"I was thinking of the very old times, when the Romans first came here, nineteen hundred years ago. They sailed up the river Thames to a dark and wild place, with bad weather, bad food and death hiding all around them. But the Romans were strong enough to face the darkness. They were conquerors[1]. They just took what they could get.

Conquest[2] is not a nice thing when you look at it too closely: it is robbery[3] and murder[4] on a large scale[5]. Conquerors, of course have the idea that conquest is something noble, that has real meaning."

Marlow broke off[6]. We watched the lights on the river, waiting patiently for him to continue. After a long silence, Marlow went on[7], "I once sailed up a big river," and we knew that he wanted to tell us one of his long inconclusive[8] stories.

Marlow began his story.

I don't want to bother you too much with what happened to me personally. But in order to[9] understand the effect[10] this journey had on me, you need to know a number of things: how I got there, what I saw, and how I went up that river to the place where I first met Kurtz.

---

1 conqueror ['kɑŋkərə] (n.) 征服者
2 conquest ['kɑŋkwɛst] (n.) 征服；佔領
3 robbery ['rɑbərı] (n.) 搶劫
4 murder ['mɝdə] (n.) 殺害
5 on a large scale 大規模地
6 break off 停止講話

7 go on 繼續説
8 inconclusive [ˌɪnkən'klusɪv] (a.) 無結論的；不確定的
9 in order to 為了……
10 effect [ɪ'fɛkt] (n.) 作用；影響

A good story

- Which of these elements are important for you in a story? Tick (✓).

☐ Background and description.
☐ Good plot with lots of action.
☐ Satisfactory ending.
☐ Hidden meaning and moral[11].
☐ Convincing[12] characters.

I was hanging around London, resting before looking for[13] my next job. At first I wanted to go back to sea, but I couldn't find a ship. Then one day I saw a map in a shop window that I had seen as a boy. It was a map of a big dark area near the equator[14] with a huge river in its center. I decided that I wanted to go there: to Africa.

I remembered there was a foreign company that traded on the Congo River, and that I had an aunt who knew one of the bosses of that same company. And so thanks to my aunt I got a job with the company as the captain of a river steamboat[15].

11 moral [ˈmɔrəl] (n.) 寓意；道德上的教訓
12 convincing [kənˈvɪnsɪŋ] (a.) 使人信服的
13 look for 尋找
14 equator [ɪˈkwetɚ] (n.) 赤道
15 steamboat [ˈstimbot] (n.) 汽船

Within forty-eight hours I was crossing the Channel[1] to meet my employers[2] in Belgium and sign the contract[3]. While I was there I was also asked to have a medical[4] in which a little old doctor took my pulse[5] and measured my head. I thought this was strange and I asked him why this was important.

"The biggest change to the men who go to Africa happens inside their heads," he said mysteriously[6].

He then asked me if there was a history of madness[7] in my family. This annoyed[8] me greatly and I told him so.

Just remember to avoid[9] getting angry when you are out there. In the tropics[10], anger can be more dangerous than the sun. Keep calm. Calm. Goodbye," he said before signaling[11] for me to leave.

Before starting my job I went to thank my aunt. She was very kind to me and she seemed to think I was some kind of "taker of light", going out to Africa to help "those ignorant[12] millions change their horrible ways and bring them civilization[13]."

I reminded her, however, that I was actually going to work for a company that was interested in profit[14].

I felt that I was going, not to the center of a continent[15], but to the center of the earth.

1 Channel 在這裡指英吉利海峽（English Channel）
2 employer [ɪmˋplɔɪɚ] (n.) 雇主
3 contract [ˋkɑntrækt] (n.) 契約
4 medical [ˋmɛdɪkḷ] (n.) 健康檢查
5 take one's pulse 量脈搏
6 mysteriously [mɪsˋtɪrɪəslɪ] (adv.) 神祕地
7 madness [ˋmædnɪs] (n.) 精神錯亂
8 annoy [əˋnɔɪ] (v.) 惹惱
9 avoid [əˋvɔɪd] (v.) 避開
10 the tropics 熱帶地區
11 signal [ˋsɪgnḷ] (v.) 以動作示意
12 ignorant [ˋɪgnərənt] (a.) 無知的
13 civilization [ˌsɪvḷəˋzeʃən] (n.) 文明
14 profit [ˋprɑfɪt] (n.) 利潤
15 continent [ˋkɑntənənt] (n.) 大陸；大洲

Conquest/colonization

- Where is Marlow going?

- What nationality is the company he now works for?

- Marlow talks about the Roman conquest of Britain.
  Look up the word **"conquest"** in a dictionary.
  Marlow decides to work for a European company
  that trades in Africa. What do you know about the
  European colonization of Africa? Look up the word
  "colonization" in a dictionary.

- What is the difference between conquest and
  colonization? Discuss in groups.

1 edge [ɛdʒ] (n.) 邊緣
2 wilderness [ˈwɪldənɪs] (n.) 荒野
3 glittering [ˈglɪtərɪŋ] (a.) 閃閃發光的
4 paddle [ˈpædl] (v.) 划槳行進
5 momentary [ˈmomənˌtɛrɪ] (a.) 短暫的
6 come upon 偶然遇到

7 apparent [əˈpærənt] (a.) 顯而易見的
8 dig up 挖掘
9 jetty [ˈdʒɛtɪ]
  (n.) 突碼頭；
  防波堤

Chapter 2

I left in a French steamboat. We followed the coast of Africa which seemed like the edge[1] of a wilderness[2]. The dark green jungle was almost black beside the glittering[3] sea. Sometimes we saw black-skinned men paddling[4] a boat; they were a great comfort to look at, a momentary[5] contact with reality. Once we came upon[6] a French ship, anchored off the coast, firing into the jungle with heavy guns for no apparent[7] reason.

It was more than thirty days before we got to the mouth of the big river. I then changed boat and traveled up the river on a smaller steamer with a young Swedish captain. He told me that he had recently taken another Swedish sailor up the river, but he had killed himself on the way.

When I asked why, he answered: "Who knows? The sun was too much for him, or the country perhaps."

At last we arrived at a place where the earth was all dug up[8], and a lot of people, mostly black and wearing skins, were moving about like ants. There were houses on a hill, and a jetty[9] projected into the river.

"There's your company's station," said the Swedish captain, pointing to three wooden buildings on the rocky hill. "I will send your things up. Goodbye."

I walked up the path towards the station. The black workers were building a railway. There were pieces of broken machinery[1] everywhere and rusty rails. Every now and then the natives[2] ran to take cover and an explosion[3] shook the ground. These explosions seemed to be the only proper work that was going on.

I saw dark shapes lying in the shade. I soon realized that they were exhausted[4] workers who had come to escape[5] the sun and were now waiting to die. They stared vacantly[6] at nothing, lying in unnatural positions. I stood and looked at them in horror, then hurried away towards the station.

Near the buildings I met a white man, who I found out later was the company's chief accountant[7]. He seemed like a vision! He was immaculately[8] dressed in white. He was wearing a clean shirt and necktie, jacket, white trousers and polished boots. His hair was parted neatly and brushed. I shook hands with him.

The accountant and his books[9] were in perfect order—he had trained a native woman to look after him and his clothes in the three years he had been there.

But everything else was disorganized[10]—people, things, buildings. Strings[11] of natives arrived and departed. They took with them a stream[12] of rubbishy[13] cottons, beads and brass wire into the depths of the jungle, further down the river. In return they brought a precious trickle[14] of ivory to the station.

Trade

- What is the company trading in and where?
- What do you know about this product and its trade? Discuss in groups.

I had to spend ten days at this outer trading station, which seemed like an eternity[15]. I spent some of the time in the accountant's hot wooden office. Here, he sat on a high stool at his desk and wrote numbers. It was he who first spoke to me of Kurtz.

One day he remarked[16], without lifting his head, "In the interior you will no doubt meet Kurtz."

On asking, I was told that Kurtz was a first-class agent, and a very remarkable person. He was in charge of a very important trading-post[17], in the true ivory country. He collected as much ivory as all the other agents put together.

1 machinery [mə`ʃinərɪ] (n.) 機械
2 native [`netɪv] (n.) 本地人；土著
3 explosion [ɪk`sploʒən] (n.) 爆炸
4 exhausted [ɪg`zɔstɪd] (a.) 精疲力竭的
5 escape [ə`skep] (v.) 逃跑；逃避
6 vacantly [`vekəntlɪ] (adv.) 神情茫然地
7 accountant [ə`kauntənt] (n.) 會計人員
8 immaculately [ɪ`mækjəlɪtlɪ] (adv.) 乾淨地；純潔地
9 book [bʊk] (n.) 帳簿
10 disorganized [dɪs`ɔrgə͵naɪzɪd] (a.) 雜亂無章的
11 string [strɪŋ] (n.) 一串；一列
12 stream [strim] (n.) 束
13 rubbishy [`rʌbɪʃɪ] (a.) 垃圾般的
14 trickle [`trɪkl̩] (n.) 細流
15 eternity [ɪ`tɝnətɪ] (n.) 永恆
16 remark [rɪ`mɑrk] (v.) 談論
17 trading-post [`tredɪŋ͵post] (n.) 商棧；貿易站

"When you see Kurtz," he went on, "tell him from me that everything here is very satisfactory. I don't like to write to him because you never know who might get hold of[1] the letter at the Central Station." He paused, looking at me for a moment. "Oh, Kurtz will go very far[2]," he continued. "He will become important in the administration[3] before long. They—the bosses in Europe, you know—intend him to become important."

Career

- Why does the accountant think that Kurtz will go far?
- What does the expression "go far" mean for you? Tell a friend.

The next day I left the station, with a caravan[4] of sixty men, each with a massive load[5], for the three-hundred mile walk.

We went on a network of paths, through long grass, through burnt grass, through bushes, up and down stony hills in burning heat; and there was a great solitude[6]. The population had long gone[7] and we passed through empty villages.

I had a fat white companion who at first kept fainting[8] in the heat, so I had to shade him with my own coat. I couldn't help but ask why he had gone there.

---

1 get hold of 掌握；取得
2 go far 有成就
3 administration [əd,mɪnə`streʃən] (n.) 管理階層
4 caravan [`kærə,væn] (n.) 商隊
5 load [lod] (n.) 裝載
6 solitude [`sɑlə,tjud] (n.) 荒涼 (之地)
7 long gone 離開許久
8 faint [fent] (v.) 昏厥

🎧12   "To make money, of course," he replied.

Then he got a fever and had to be carried, which caused arguments with the carriers because of his weight.

After fifteen days, we arrived at the Central Station. It was on a backwater[1] of the big river, surrounded[2] by scrub[3] and forest.

Another fat white man—one of several agents with long sticks who had come to examine me—told me that my steamer was at the bottom of the river. He said I should go and see the general manager[4] immediately. Apparently, a volunteer[5] captain had broken the bottom of the boat on some stones, and the steamer had sunk near the south bank. The work of raising[6] the boat out of the river and repairing it was to take me several months.

The manager was an unremarkable[7] man to look at, with cold blue eyes. He was obeyed, but not out of love, fear or respect. It was more to do with the power he had gained by being there. He was a common[8] trader who had managed to[9] stay healthy for three years. This was very unusual out here. He was not good at organization, initiative[10] or order. That was obvious[11] from things such as the terrible state of the station. He had no learning or intelligence[12]. He kept the routine[13] going. That was all.

Despite[14] my thirty-mile walk that morning, the manager started telling me things as soon as he saw me. The up-river station had to be relieved[15]. There had been many delays already. They did not know who was dead and who was alive, or how they were—and so on, and so on. There were rumors that a very important station was in danger, and that its chief, Kurtz, was ill. He was very worried. He asked how long it would take to get the boat repaired.

"How can I tell?" I said. "I haven't even seen it yet—probably a few months."

"Well, let's say three months," he said. "That should be enough time. Then you can travel up to Kurtz."

I walked out of his hut[16], muttering[17] to myself my opinion of him. He was an idiot. I took it back later, however, when it turned out that three months was exactly how long the work of repairing the boat required.

I went down to the river to see the boat the next day. I looked back at the station and saw the company's agents with their absurd[18] long sticks walking around in the sunshine. The word "ivory" rang in the air; it was whispered and sighed. It was almost as if the agents were praying. I've never seen anything so unreal in my life. The only real thing, perhaps, was their desire to get appointed to a trading-post where ivory was to be found, so that they could earn percentages[19].

And outside, the silent wilderness surrounding this activity seemed great and unbeatable[20], like evil or truth, waiting patiently for this invasion[21] to disappear.

---

1 backwater [ˈbæk‚wɔtə] (n.) 逆流水
2 surround [səˈraund] (v.) 圍繞
3 scrub [skrʌb] (n.) 矮樹叢
4 general manager 總經理
5 volunteer [‚valənˈtɪr] (n.) 自願參加者
6 raise [rez] (v.) 拉起
7 unremarkable [‚ʌnrɪˈmarkəbl̩] (a.) 平凡的
8 common [ˈkamən] (a.) 普通的
9 manage to 成功地設法
10 initiative [ɪˈnɪʃətɪv]
     (n.) 主動的行動；進取心
11 obvious [ˈabvɪəs] (a.) 明顯的
12 intelligence [ɪnˈtɛlədʒəns] (n.) 才智
13 routine [ruˈtin] (n.) 例行公事
14 despite [dɪˈspaɪt] (prep.) 儘管
15 relieve [rɪˈliv] (v.) 接替；解除
16 hut [hʌt] (n.) 臨時營房；小屋
17 mutter [ˈmʌtə] (v.) 低聲嘀咕
18 absurd [əbˈsɝd] (a.) 荒謬的
19 percentage [pəˈsɛntɪdʒ] (n.) 利潤
20 unbeatable [ʌnˈbitəbl̩] (a.) 無敵的
21 invasion [ɪnˈveʒən] (n.) 侵略；侵佔

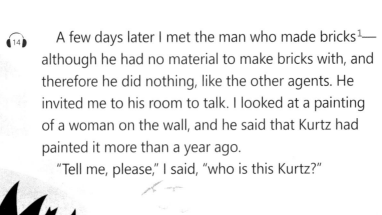

A few days later I met the man who made bricks[1]—
although he had no material to make bricks with, and
therefore he did nothing, like the other agents. He
invited me to his room to talk. I looked at a painting
of a woman on the wall, and he said that Kurtz had
painted it more than a year ago.

"Tell me, please," I said, "who is this Kurtz?"

"The chief of the Inner Station," he answered. "A prodigy[2]. Today he is the chief of the best station, next year he will be assistant manager[3], two years more and . . . But I expect you know what he will be. You are part of the new group. The same people who sent him recommended you. I know."

What he said was so far from the truth that I nearly started laughing—my aunt's influential[4] friends were producing some strange effects on others.

What I needed to do my job was rivets[5]. They had boxes of them down at the coast. But we had none here. We had metal[6] plates[7] for the repairs, but nothing to fasten[8] them with, so I could not get on with the work and close the hole in the boat.

While we waited I had plenty of time to meditate[9] on Kurtz. I wasn't very interested in him. Still, I was curious to see whether this man, who had come here with moral ideas of some sort, would climb to the top after all, and how he would set about[10] his work when he got there.

Stations

- What do you notice about the different names for the stations?

1 brick [brɪk] (n.) 磚
2 prodigy [ˈprɑdədʒɪ] (n.) 奇才
3 assistant manager 協理
4 influential [ˌɪnfluˈɛnʃəl] (a.) 有影響的
5 rivet [ˈrɪvɪt] (n.) 鉚釘
6 metal [ˈmɛtl̩] (n.) (a.) 金屬 (的)
7 plate [plet] (n.) 盤；板
8 fasten [ˈfæsn̩] (v.) 閂住
9 meditate [ˈmɛdəˌtet] (v.) 深入思考
10 set about 著手做某事

(15)   One evening I was lying flat on the deck[1] of my steamboat when I overheard[2] the manager speaking to one of his colleagues about Kurtz.

I understood that Kurtz had asked to be sent to that particular station to show the administration what he could do. He had come three hundred miles down the river with his assistant and the ivory to the headquarters[3]. But Kurtz had then turned and gone back to his station, saying that he preferred to work alone.

The two men I overheard talking were amazed[4] that anyone would have done that. And for the first time I felt I could really imagine what Kurtz was like. A lone white man, turning his back on the headquarters and his colleagues, and paddling back in his canoe[5] with four natives, to his empty and desolate[6] station in the wilderness.

The assistant had told the manager that Kurtz had been very ill, and had only partly recovered[7]. It seemed that there had been no other news since then, and that was nine months ago. And there had been no more ivory, either.

"It's not my fault!" said the manager at this point.

"Very sad," said his fat colleague.

16 "And he was such a problem when he was here, too. He said things like: 'Each station must be like a light on the road to better things. A center for trade, of course, but also for improving[8] the natives and instructing them.' Imagine! And he wants to be a manager himself!"

Some time later, the fat trader I had traveled there with left the headquarters and went into the wilderness with his group, and we heard no more of them.

We were to leave soon, too, and go towards Kurtz's station. I was very excited at the thought of meeting Kurtz, although it actually took us two months from the day we left the headquarters until we came to the bank below Kurtz's station.

Anticipation

- Why do you think Marlow is excited to meet Kurtz?
- Have you ever heard so much about someone that you are excited to meet them?

1 deck [dɛk] (n.) 甲板
2 overhear [ˌovɚˋhɪr] (v.) 無意中聽到（三態：overhear; overheard; overheard）
3 headquarters [ˋhɛdˋkwɔrtɚz] (n.) 總部
4 amazed [əˋmezd] (a.) 吃驚的
5 canoe [kəˋnu] (n.) 獨木舟
6 desolate [ˋdɛsḷət] (a.) 荒蕪的
7 recover [rɪˋkʌvɚ] (v.) 恢復
8 improve [ɪmˋpruv] (v.) 改善

Going up that river was like traveling back to the earliest beginnings of the world, when vegetation[1] was everywhere on earth and big trees were kings. An empty river, a great silence, an impenetrable[2] forest. The air was warm, thick and heavy. There was no pleasure to be had from the brilliant[3] sunshine. The water just ran on, deserted[4], into the shadowy distance[5]. On silvery sandbanks lay hippos and alligators, side by side. Often the river was broken up by a series of small islands, and it was difficult to find the main channel to sail along. I had to watch at all times, for fear of hitting the bottom of the steamboat on the banks that were hidden under the water.

And then there were the continual repairs that had to be made to broken steam pipes. I was so busy that I often forgot where I was, but I felt it all the same; I felt as if the mysterious stillness[6] was watching me.

As well as the manager, I also had three or four of the white agents from headquarters on board, and there were about twenty cannibals[7] as my crew[8]. They often had to jump out and help push and pull the boat along where the water was too shallow to sail. I also had a fireman[9]. He was a native who had been trained to watch the water gauge[10]. He knew that if the level of water was too low, the boiler[11] might explode[12]. So he sweated and watched the gauge fearfully.

---

1 vegetation [ˌvɛdʒəˈteʃən]
  (n.)（總稱）植物；草木
2 impenetrable [ɪmˈpɛnətrəbl̩]
  (a.) 不能穿過的
3 brilliant [ˈbrɪljənt] (a.) 明亮的
4 deserted [dɪˈzɝtɪd] (a.) 遺棄的
5 distance [ˈdɪstəns] (n.) 距離；遠處
6 stillness [ˈstɪlnɪs] (n.) 靜止不動

7 cannibal [ˈkænəbl̩] (n.) 食人者
8 crew [kru] (n.) 一組工作人員
9 fireman [ˈfaɪrmən]
  (n.)（蒸汽機等的）火伕
10 gauge [gedʒ] (n.) 測量儀器
11 boiler [ˈbɔɪlə] (n.) 鍋爐；汽鍋
12 explode [ɪkˈsplod] (v.) 爆炸

Sometimes we came upon a small station where a few white men came rushing out full of joy and surprise and welcome; then the word "ivory" rang in the air before we went on again into the silence.

The empty water and trees, trees, trees, millions of trees, enormous[1], huge and high. And the little steamboat crawling[2] through it all. It made you feel very small, very lost.

Where the others imagined they were going to, I do not know. To some place where they expected to get something, I suppose. For me we were crawling towards Kurtz—exclusively[3], as we penetrated[4] further and further into the heart of darkness.

Expedition[5]

- Who is on the steamer and where are they going?

It was very quiet, but at night sometimes there were drums from amongst the trees. The sound seemed to hang in the air above our heads until the first light of day. Nobody knew whether these drums meant war, peace or prayer.

Sometimes we found a native village, with reed-walled[6] houses with pointed grass roofs, and there was a sudden movement of black arms and legs, a mass of hands clapping, feet stamping and bodies moving on the bank. They howled[7] and leaped and spun[8], and made frightening faces.

1 enormous [ɪˈnɔrməs] (a.) 巨大的
2 crawl [krɔl] (v.) 爬行
3 exclusively [ɪkˈsklusɪvlɪ] (adv.) 唯一地
4 penetrate [ˈpɛnə͵tret] (v.) 穿入
5 expedition [͵ɛkspɪˈdɪʃən] (n.) 遠征（隊）

6 reed-walled [ˈrid͵wɔld]
    (a.) 牆是蘆葦草製成的
7 howl [haʊl] (v.) 怒吼
8 spin [spɪn] (v.) 旋轉
    （三態：spin; spun; spun）

(19) We sailed on past this incomprehensible[1] display[2]. We were cut off from any understanding of our surroundings. It was too distant from our everyday lives in the modern world. And yet, we could also relate[3] to them and what they were doing, although it was remote[4] from us. After all, they were human beings and so were we, and we all felt happiness, sadness, fear and anger in the same way.

Human beings

- Do YOU prefer silence or noise?
- Do YOU prefer stillness or movement?

About fifty miles below the Inner Station, we found a hut of reeds, a pole with a type of flag on top and a neat[5] pile of cut wood. This was unexpected. I sailed close to the bank and on the pile of firewood someone had written: "Wood for you. Hurry up. Approach[6] cautiously."

We were puzzled[7] by the message. Where should we "hurry up" to? Up the river? How could we "approach cautiously" in a noisy steamboat? What was wrong higher up the river? And how bad was the situation? What a mystery!

1 incomprehensible [ɪnˌkɑmprɪˈhɛnsəbl̩] (a.) 難以理解的
2 display [dɪˈsple] (n.) 展出
3 relate [rɪˈlet] (v.) 相關
4 remote [rɪˈmot] (a.) 遙遠的
5 neat [nit] (a.) 整潔的
6 approach [əˈprotʃ] (v.) 接近
7 puzzled [ˈpʌzl̩d] (a.) 困惑的

As we traveled on, I expected the steamboat to stop working at any moment; however by the end of the second day from the hut we were about eight miles away from Kurtz's station. I wanted to continue, but the manager said that the river was very dangerous up there, and that it would be better to wait until morning.

As we still had plenty of wood, I stopped the boat in the middle of the river for the night. It was in a straight stretch[8] of river with high trees on either bank. Everything was completely silent. And then night fell.

When the sun rose there was a white fog standing all around us, like something solid[9]. It lifted briefly for a few minutes at around nine o'clock showing us the river, trees and sun, but then came down again, hiding everything.

Suddenly the silence was broken; a very loud cry filled[10] the air. This was followed by the noise of many voices shouting together in a desperate[11], complaining way. Then there was a series of dramatic[12] cries. They seemed to come from all sides at once[13], but then they stopped as suddenly as they had started.

The men from headquarters rushed out of the cabins[14] with their Winchester rifles[15] ready . . . but ready for what? All we could see was the steamer we were standing on. The rest of the world had disappeared.

---

8 stretch [strɛtʃ] (n.) 伸出；延伸
9 solid [`sɑlɪd] (a.) 固體的
10 fill [fɪl] (v.) 充滿
11 desperate [`dɛspərɪt] (a.) 絕望的
12 dramatic [drə`mætɪk] (a.) 充滿激情的

13 at once 立刻
14 cabin [`kæbɪn] (n.) 船艙
15 rifle [`raɪfl] (n.) 步槍；來福槍

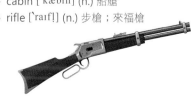

Chapter 4

I ordered the chain to be pulled up so that the anchor could be lifted easily and we could move if the fog cleared again.

"Will they attack[1]?" whispered the frightened voice of a short fat man from headquarters.

"We will all be killed in this fog," replied another.

The leader of the cannibals stood near me as his men pulled up the chain.

"Catch them," he said to me. "Catch them and give them to us."

"To you?" I asked. "What would you do with them?"

"Eat them," he replied, looking out into the fog.

Of course, I realized, he and his cannibal friends were hungry! They had only eaten some dead hippo meat they had brought with them when we started over a month ago. We hadn't stopped as planned for them to get more food on the way. They had each been given three pieces of brass[2] wire[3] about 20 cm long every week; the theory was that they would buy their food with that currency[4] in riverside villages. But that didn't work because there were either no villages, or the people were too hostile[5], or the manager didn't want to stop the boat for reasons of his own.

---

1 attack [əˋtæk] (v.) (n.) 攻擊
2 brass [bræs] (n.) (a.) 黃銅（的）
3 wire [waɪr] (n.) 金屬線
4 currency [ˋkɝənsɪ] (n.) 通貨；貨幣
5 hostile [ˋhɑstaɪl]
  (a.) 不友善的；敵意的

Apart from[1] the hippo, the only other thing I saw them eat was something which looked like half-cooked bread which they kept wrapped in leaves.

Now that I think of it, I don't know why the thirty of them hadn't killed the five of us whites and eaten us!

Cannibals

- What do you know about cannibals? Do some research on the Internet and discuss in groups.

"It is very serious," said the manager's voice behind me. "If anything happens to Kurtz before we get to him, I will be devastated[2]."

Despite what I had heard him say earlier as I lay on the deck of the steamboat, I believed he was being sincere. He was the kind of man who wanted to keep up appearances[3].

"We need to continue immediately," he said.

I didn't bother to answer him as we both knew that it was impossible.

"I authorize[4] you to take all risks," he said after a short silence.

"And I refuse to take any risks," I answered shortly.

"Well, I must accept your judgment. You are the captain," he said in a surprisingly polite way. "Will they attack, do you think?"

I did not think they would attack, for several obvious reasons. One, for the thick fog: if they left the bank in their canoes they would get lost in it, just as we would if we tried to move. Two, I believed that the jungle on either bank was impenetrable, even though there were eyes in it, eyes that had seen us. Three, during the few minutes that the fog had lifted, I had not seen any canoes anywhere.

But why I really thought they wouldn't attack was because of the *nature* of the sound they had made: it had given an impression of great sadness; the sight of our steamboat had filled these people with sorrow for some reason.

Guess

- Why do you think the sight of the steamboat has made the natives sad?

Eventually[5] the fog lifted, and we steamed up the river until we were about a mile from Kurtz's station. There was a point in the river where we had to sail very close to the bank. Some of the trees and bushes hung over the water. From my cabin on the deck I was watching everything very carefully.

---

1 apart from 除了……外
2 devastate [ˈdɛvəsˌtet]
  (v.) 破壞；毀滅
3 appearance [əˈpɪrəns]
  (n.) 外貌；表面跡象

4 authorize [ˈɔθəˌraɪz] (v.) 授權；批准
5 eventually [ɪˈvɛntʃuəlɪ]
  (n.) 最後地；終於地

🎧(24)   At the front of the ship one of the crew was checking the depth of the water with a pole; below me the fireman was putting wood into the furnace[1]; and by my side the helmsman[2] was steering[3] the boat. All of a sudden the man at the front lay down on the deck, and the fireman bent down. I was amazed.

Then I looked up and I saw that the air was full of wooden sticks flying towards us. All this time the river, the bank and the woods were very quiet, so I could hear the noise of the engine and then suddenly the patter[4] of the arrows falling everywhere. Arrows! Someone was shooting at us!

I stepped into the cabin quickly and went to close the shutters[5] on the land side. Amongst the leaves I saw faces looking at me very fiercely[6] and steadily, and as I looked more carefully I saw that the forest was full of people. And the arrows flew from them towards us. Below me on the deck the men from headquarters ran out with their Winchesters and shot into the bushes. The whole scene became confused, as smoke rose from the guns.

The helmsman grabbed[7] the rifle in the cabin, opened the shutters I had closed, and shot into the trees, but this was a mistake because somebody threw or pushed a spear[8] into his side below his ribs[9]. He sank to the floor, crying in pain.

1 furnace [ˋfɝnɪs] (n.) 火爐；熔爐
2 helmsman [ˋhɛlmzmən] (n.) 舵手
3 steer [stɪr] (v.) 掌舵
4 patter [ˋpætɚ] (n.) 啪嗒聲
5 shutters [ˋʃʌtɚz] (n.) 百葉窗
6 fiercely [ˋfɪrslɪ] (adv.) 兇猛地
7 grab [græb] (v.) 抓取
8 spear [spɪr] (n.) 矛
9 rib [rɪb] (n.) 肋骨

There was more shooting from the guns on the deck and wild screaming[1] from the men in the jungle. I took over steering the ship, and grabbed the steam whistle letting out a series of loud screeches[2].

The screaming in the forest stopped, and was followed by a long wail[3] of fear and sadness; it seemed as if the last hope had disappeared from earth. There was a great deal of movement in the bushes, and the shower of arrows stopped.

One of the agents from headquarters came up with a message from the manager, but I ignored him and made him steer the ship.

He looked at the helmsman on the floor. "He is dead," he said quietly.

"No doubt about it," I replied. "And I suppose Mr Kurtz is dead as well by this time."

I felt an extreme[4] sense[5] of disappointment. After this attack I was sure that Kurtz was already dead. I realized that I had come all this way to hear him speak, and that now I never would. It was not that he had managed to get more ivory than all the other agents together. The point was that he was a very gifted[6] man, and that his most important gift was his ability to talk— that he could express[7] himself like a stream of light.

I thought, "Good Lord! It's all over. We are too late; he has vanished[8]—the gift has vanished—he has been killed. I will never hear him speak after all."

26 Of course, I was wrong. The privilege[9] of listening to him was waiting for me. Oh, yes. And I heard more than enough.

When we arrived at Kurtz's hut, we found piles of ivory. We filled the steamboat with it, putting a lot of it on the deck. It was his. Everything was his.

Kurtz talked like that: "My ivory, my station, my river, my Intended[10], my . . ." Everything belonged to him—but the thing I wanted to know was what he belonged to—what powers of darkness had taken him? What had changed him? Kurtz was obviously no longer the man I had heard about.

And Kurtz told me a lot before he died. This was because he was happy to speak English again after being alone with the natives for so long. He also showed me a report he had written on how the cruel traditions of the African natives could be stopped, "The Suppression[11] of Savage[12] Customs[13]'. This report was seventeen pages of writing. (I have to point out that he had completed this report before his—let us say—nerves[14], went wrong and he started to take part in[15] certain midnight dances that ended with the most terrible ceremonies[16].)

---

1 scream [skrim] (v.) 尖叫
2 screech [skritʃ] (n.) 尖銳刺耳的聲音
3 wail [wel] (n.) 慟哭聲
4 extreme [ɪkˋstrim] (a.) 極端的；極度的
5 sense [sɛns] (n.) 感覺
6 gifted [ˋgɪftɪd] (a.) 有天賦的
7 express [ɪkˋsprɛs] (v.) 表達
8 vanish [ˋvænɪʃ] (v.) 消失
9 privilege [ˋprɪvlɪdʒ] (n.) 特權；優待

10 Intended [ɪnˋtɛndɪd] (n.) 已訂婚者
11 suppression [səˋprɛʃən] (n.) 壓迫
12 savage [ˋsævɪdʒ] (a.) 野蠻的
       (n.) 野蠻人
13 customs [ˋkʌstəmz] (n.) 社會習俗
14 nerve [nɝv] (n.) 神經
15 take part in 參加⋯⋯
16 ceremony [ˋsɛrə͵monɪ] (n.) 儀式

When I read the report, I was impressed by the way it was written—his language was eloquent[1] and his words noble and passionate[2]. But the whole thing led to a terrible conclusion[3]: the only way to stop the traditions was to exterminate[4] all the natives!

He begged me to take good care of his report.

Powers of darkness

- What do you think went wrong for Kurtz?
- What do you think the darkness represents?

But I am jumping ahead in my story. After the attack, we sailed the short distance to the station where we were met by a white man wearing brightly patched[5] clothes. He came on board the steamboat.

"I don't like this," I said to the man. "The natives are in the jungle."

"They are simple people," he said. "I am glad you came. It took me all my time to keep them away."

He then started talking quickly about the boat and the people, as if he hadn't talked to anyone for a long time.

---

1 eloquent [ˈɛləkwənt] (a.) 雄辯的；有說服力的
2 passionate [ˈpæʃənɪt] (a.) 熱烈的；激昂的
3 conclusion [kənˈkluʒən] (n.) 結論
4 exterminate [ɪkˈstɜːməˌnet] (v.) 滅絕
5 patched [ˈpætʃɪd] (a.) 補釘的

"Don't you talk to Kurtz?" I asked.

"You don't talk to that man," he replied. "You listen to him."

I then asked him to tell me about himself. He was a Russian sailor, and had been sent into the jungle by a Dutch trading company. He explained that the house where we had found the wood had been his.

"I had lots of trouble to keep these people away," he said.

"Did they want to kill you?" I asked.

"Oh, no!" he cried.

"Why did they attack us?" I continued.

"They don't want Kurtz to go," he answered after a pause[1].

"Don't they?" I said curiously.

And he nodded a mysterious nod. "I tell you—this man has enlarged[2] my mind," he said, opening his arms wide.

---

1 pause [pɔz] (n.) 暫停；中斷
2 enlarge [ɪnˈlɑrdʒ] (v.) 擴大
3 exist [ɪgˈzɪst] (v.) 生存
4 remain [rɪˈmen] (v.) 逗留
5 audience [ˈɔdɪəns] (n.) 聽眾
6 camp [kæmp] (v.) 露營
7 probably [ˈprɑbəblɪ] (adv.) 可能地
8 explore [ɪkˈsplor] (v.) 探測；探索

Chapter 5

I looked at the Russian in his colorful clothes, and wondered how he had existed[3], how he had succeeded in coming so far down the river and how he had managed to remain[4] here.

"I went a little farther," he said, "and then a little farther—till I had gone so far that I don't know how to get back. Never mind. Plenty of time. I can manage. You take Kurtz away quickly— quickly, I tell you!"

He told me about his time with Kurtz. I suppose that Kurtz wanted an audience[5], because one time when they had camped[6] together in the forest, they had talked all night, or more probably[7] Kurtz had talked.

"We talked about everything," he said, excited by his memories. "I forgot there was such a thing as sleep. Everything! Of love, too. He made me see things."

"And have you been with him ever since?" I asked.

"No, he likes to wander alone and he often goes off into the depths of the forest," he replied.

"Does he go exploring[8]?" I asked.

He told me that Kurtz had discovered lots of villages, a lake, too—he did not know exactly in what directions—but that his expeditions had been for ivory.

🎧 30

"To speak plainly, he raided[1] the country," I suggested.
He nodded.

"Not alone, surely?" I asked. "Kurtz got the tribe[2] to follow him, didn't he?"

"They adored[3] him." he said.

By the way that he said this, I could see that Kurtz filled his life, occupied[4] his thoughts, changed his emotions[5].

"What can you expect?" he shouted. "He came to them with thunder and lightning—his guns. They had never seen anything like it. He could be very terrible. You can't judge Kurtz as you would an ordinary[6] man. No, no, no! He said he would shoot me unless I gave him my ivory because nothing could stop him from doing as he pleased. And that was true, too. I gave him the ivory. What did I care? But I didn't leave. No, no. I couldn't leave him. I had to be careful, of course, until we got friendly again. He was living for the most part in those villages by the lake. When he came down to the river, sometimes he got angry with me, and it was better for me to be careful. This man suffered[7] too much. He hated this place, but he couldn't get away. When I had a chance, I begged him to try and leave while there was time; I offered[8] to go back with him. And he said yes, and then he remained to go off on another ivory hunt, or disappear for weeks and forget himself amongst these people."

"Why, he's mad!" I said.

---

1 raid [red] (v.) 突襲
2 tribe [traɪb] (n.) 部落
3 adore [əˈdor] (v.) 崇拜；崇敬
4 occupy [ˈɑkjəˌpaɪ] (v.) 佔據
5 emotion [ɪˈmoʃən] (n.) 情感
6 ordinary [ˈɔrdnˌɛrɪ] (a.) 一般的

Kurtz

- What do we learn about Kurtz from the Russian? Work with a partner.

He protested[9] strongly. Kurtz couldn't be mad. He was such a great talker and was a brilliant man. But it appeared, from what the Russian said, that Kurtz's appetite[10] for more ivory had gradually changed his view of what was the right or wrong way to get it.

The Russian then explained that Kurtz had suddenly become quite ill. "I heard he was lying helpless, and so I came up here—I took my chance," he said. "Oh, he is bad, very bad."

There were no signs of life up at Kurtz's house on the hill, with its ruined roof, long mud wall and three little square windows of different sizes.

I looked at it again through my telescope[11], and saw something which shocked me.

The top of each post in the fence around the buildings had the remains of a human head on it. I realized that these heads showed that Kurtz had a lack of restraint[12], that he would do anything when he needed to. His morality and vision had been lost in the wilderness.

---

7 suffer [ˈsʌfɚ] (v.) 遭受；受苦
8 offer [ˈɔfɚ] (v.) 提供
9 protest [prəˈtɛst] (v.) 抗議；反對
10 appetite [ˈæpəˌtaɪt] (n.) 胃口
11 telescope [ˈtɛləˌskop] (n.)（單筒）望遠鏡
12 restraint [rɪˈstrent] (n.) 抑制

The Russian told me that he did not dare[1] to take the heads down. He was not afraid of the natives; they never did anything until Kurtz gave the word. Kurtz's power was extraordinary[2]. The natives' camps surrounded the place, and the chiefs came to see him every day. He started to describe how they approached Kurtz, but I stopped him.

"I don't want to know anything about the ceremonies used when approaching Kurtz," I shouted.

I somehow found such details more unacceptable than the heads drying on the fence posts. The Russian seemed surprised by my attitude towards Kurtz.

"I don't understand," the Russian said. "I've been doing my best to keep him alive. I have nothing to do with the heads—they were rebels[3]—or the ceremonies. There has been no medicine[4] or decent[5] food here for months. Kurtz was shamefully[6] abandoned[7]. A man like this, with such ideas . . ."

Suddenly round the corner of Kurtz's house a group of men appeared, walking through the tall grass and carrying a stretcher[8]. Instantly, there was a loud cry which cut through the air like a sharp arrow.

1 dare [dɛr] (v.) 竟敢
2 extraordinary [ɪkˋstrɔrdṇˏɛrɪ] (a.) 特別的
3 rebel [ˋrɛbəl] (n.) 造反者
4 medicine [ˋmɛdəsṇ] (n.) 醫藥
5 decent [ˋdisṇt] (a.) 像樣的

6 shamefully [ˋʃemfəlɪ] (adv.) 不名譽地
7 abandon [əˋbændən] (v.) 遺棄
8 stretcher [ˋstrɛtʃɚ] (n.) 擔架

As if by magic, streams of people appeared, with spears in their hands, with bows, with shields and with wild glances[1] and violent looks. They poured into the open area below the house, and then everything was still.

"Now if Kurtz doesn't say the right thing to them we are all finished," said the Russian, who was watching by my side.

The men carrying the stretcher stopped halfway towards the steamer where we were, and the man lying on it sat up.

"Let us hope that the man who can talk so well of love will find a good reason to save us," I said.

I looked through my telescope and saw Kurtz with his thin arm held up above him commandingly[2], his mouth moving in speech, though we could hear nothing.

He fell back suddenly, and the men with the stretcher moved forward again. At the same time, I noticed that the crowds were vanishing back into the forest as quickly as they had appeared.

Some of the men from headquarters were walking behind the stretcher carrying Kurtz's guns. The manager was walking beside the stretcher, talking to him.

They laid him down in one of the little cabins on the steamboat which had just enough room for the bed and two small camp stools. We had brought his correspondence[3], and the bed was covered with many open letters and papers.

He held up one of the letters and looked straight at me, saying: "I am glad'.

---

1 glance [glæns] (n.) 掃視
2 commandingly [kə`mændɪŋlɪ] (adv.) 命令式地
3 correspondence [ˌkɔrə`spɑndəns] (n.) （總稱）信件

(34) Someone had obviously written to him about me. I was struck[1] by his voice, which was serious, deep and full, while he looked so ill and incapable[2] of more than a whisper!

Expectations

- Marlow still hasn't "met" Kurtz but he already knows a lot about him.
- Have you ever known a lot about someone before you actually met them?
- Did that person fulfill[3] your expectations or were they very different from how you imagined them to be?

The manager appeared in the doorway and I stepped out to where the Russian and the men from headquarters were standing. I followed the direction that they were looking in. Dark, human shapes were visible, moving around the gloomy edges of the forest.

Near the river stood two bronze[4] figures[5], leaning on tall spears and wearing fantastic[6] head-dresses of spotted skins, warlike and quiet at the same time. And from right to left along the sunny bank, moved a wild and gorgeous[7] woman.

---

1 strike [straɪk] (v.) 打動；感動（三態：strike; struck; struck, stricken）
2 incapable [ɪnˈkepəbl̩] (a.) 無能的
3 fulfill [fʊlˈfɪl] (v.) 實現

4 bronze [brɑnz] (n.) (a.) 古銅色（的）
5 figure [ˈfɪgjɚ] (n.) 體形；人物
6 fantastic [fænˈtæstɪk] (a.) 奇異的
7 gorgeous [ˈgɔrdʒəs] (a.) 美麗的

She walked in a slow and proud way, jingling[1] with metal ornaments at each step. She held her head high; her hair was done into the shape of a helmet[2]; she had brass leggings[3] to her knee, brass gloves to her elbow, and dark red spots on each cheek. Around her neck were many necklaces with glass beads that shook and glittered[4] at every step. She was savage and superb[5] and there was something dangerous in her slow, continuous movements.

She came to the side of the steamer, stood still and faced us. Her face had a mixture of sadness, fear and pain.

There was a terrible silence around us.

Then she turned away slowly and walked on, following the river bank, only turning once to stare at us for a moment, before she disappeared into the forest.

"If she had tried to come on board," said the Russian, "I think I would have shot her. I have been risking my life every day for the last fortnight[6] to keep her out of the house. She got in one time and talked loudly to Kurtz for an hour, turning and pointing at me frequently. I don't understand the dialect[7] of this tribe. Luckily for me, Kurtz was too ill to care that day, or I think I would have been in trouble. I don't understand. It's too much for me. Ah, well, it's all over now."

---

1 jingle [ˈdʒɪŋɡl̩] (v.) 發出叮噹聲
2 helmet [ˈhɛlmɪt] (n.) 頭盔
3 legging [ˈlɛɡɪŋ] (n.) 綁腿
4 glitter [ˈɡlɪtɚ] (v.) 閃閃發光

5 superb [suˈpɝb] (a.) 堂皇的；一流的
6 fortnight [ˈfɔrtˌnaɪt] (n.) 十四天；兩星期
7 dialect [ˈdaɪəlɛkt] (n.) 方言
8 interfere [ˌɪntɚˈfɪr] (v.) 妨礙

At that moment I heard Kurtz's deep voice from the cabin. "Save me! Save the ivory, you mean. Don't talk about saving me when I've had to save you! You are interrupting my plans now. Sick? Not so sick as you would like to think. Never mind. I'll continue with my plans—I will return. I'll show you what can be done. You with your small business ideas—you are interfering[8] with me. I will return."

The manager came out. He took my arm and we walked to the side of the boat.

"He is very low," he said. "We have done all we could for him, haven't we? But you cannot hide the fact that Kurtz has done more harm than good for the company. He was too aggressive[9] in his work. Carefully, slowly, that's my way. We must be careful. This district[10] is closed to us for a time. I don't say that there isn't a remarkable quantity[11] of ivory, and we must save it all. But look how dangerous the situation is—and why? Because his method was not good. He has no judgment. I will have to make a report about it to the company directors[12]."

"Nevertheless[13]," I said, "I think Kurtz is a remarkable man."

"He *was,*" answered the manager, and he walked away from me.

He obviously thought I was as bad as Kurtz, and believed in methods[14] which were not good. I was on the wrong side[15].

---

9 aggressive [əˋgrɛsɪv] (a.) 躁進的；挑釁的
10 district [ˋdɪstrɪkt] (n.) 區
11 quantity [ˋkwɑntətɪ] (n.) 數量
12 director [dəˋrɛktə˚] (n.) 主管
13 nevertheless [͵nɛvə˚ðəˋlɛs] (adv.) 不過；然而
14 method [ˋmɛθəd] (n.) 方法
15 on the wrong side 選錯邊站

The Russian tapped[1] me on the shoulder. "I think these white men do not like me." he said.

"You're right", I replied. "Perhaps you had better[2] go if you have any friends amongst these native people."

"Plenty," he replied. "They are simple people—and I don't want anything from them. But I don't want anything to happen to these white men, and I am worried about Kurtz's reputation[3]. I only told you what I did because we are both sailors."

"All right," I said, after a time. "Kurtz's reputation is safe with me."

He then told me in a low voice that it was Kurtz who had ordered the attack to be made on the steamer.

"He hated the idea of being taken away from here," he went on. "He wanted to scare you away[4]. I could not stop him. Oh, I had an awful time this last month."

"Thanks," I said. "I shall keep my eyes open."

"I have a canoe and three natives waiting not very far away. I am going. Could you give me some cartridges[5] for my gun, please? And a pair of shoes."

I gave him the cartridges and found an old pair of shoes for him.

"Ah! I'll never, ever meet such a man again. You should have heard him recite poetry[6]—it was his own, he told me. Poetry! Oh, he enlarged my mind."

"Goodbye," I said.

We shook hands and he vanished into the night.

Chapter 6

When I woke up just after midnight, I could see a big fire burning on the hill near the house, and other flames[7] flickered[8] in the forest where Kurtz's adorers were waiting. I could hear the slow beating of a drum and the chanting[9] of many voices. I glanced into the little cabin. A light was burning, but Kurtz was not there.

I didn't believe it at first—it seemed impossible. I realized that this meant we might be attacked at any moment, but I didn't raise the alarm, or tell any of the company agents who were sleeping on the deck.

It had become my job not to betray[10] Kurtz. I had made my choice and chose the nightmare of being on his side.

I got down off the steamer and onto the bank and saw a trail[11] through the long grass; it was obvious that Kurtz was crawling away.

I eventually found him. He got up—long, pale and unsteady[12].

"Go away—hide yourself," he said in his deep voice.

---

1 tap [tæp] (v.) 輕拍
2 had better 最好⋯⋯
  （後面一律接原形動詞）
3 reputation [ˌrɛpjəˈteʃən] (n.) 名譽
4 scare sb away 嚇跑某人
5 cartridge [ˈkɑrtrɪdʒ] (n.) 子彈
6 poetry [ˈpoɪtrɪ] (n.)（總稱）詩

7 flame [flem] (n.) 火焰
8 flicker [ˈflɪkɚ] (v.) 閃爍；搖曳
9 chant [tʃænt] (v.) 唱；吟誦
10 betray [bɪˈtre] (v.) 背叛；出賣
11 trail [trel] (n.) 小道
12 unsteady [ʌnˈstɛdɪ] (a.) 不穩定的

"Do you know what you are doing?" I whispered.

"Perfectly," he answered, raising his voice.

"You will be lost," I said. "Completely lost."

"I had immense[1] plans," he muttered. "I was going to do great things. And now because of this stupid manager . . ."

"Your success in Europe is certain, whatever happens," I said, trying to appeal to[2] something that was important to him.

I knew that there was nothing above or below him. Kurtz was alone. I watched as he struggled[3] with his own desires and hopes. I realized the terrible danger, because he could easily call the natives to kill us all. I had tried to break the spell of the wilderness that seemed to hold him so tightly.

Believe me or not, his intelligence was perfectly clear—concentrated[4], it is true, upon himself with horrible intensity[5], yet clear. This was my only chance: to appeal to his intelligence. (The other option[6] was to kill him there and then, which wasn't so good, because of the noise it would make.)

But his soul was mad. Being alone in the wilderness, it had looked within itself, and, by heavens! I tell you, it had gone mad. And now it was my turn to look into his soul, too. He was eloquent and sincere until the end. He struggled with himself, too. I saw it, I heard it. I saw the inconceivable[7] mystery of a soul that knew no restraint, no faith[8], and no fear, yet struggled blindly with itself.

---

1 immense [ɪˈmɛns] (a.) 無限的

2 appeal to 訴諸於……

3 struggle [ˈstrʌɡl̩] (v.) 掙扎

4 concentrated [ˈkɑnsɛn͵tretɪd] (a.) 專注的

5 intensity [ɪnˈtɛnsətɪ] (n.)（思想的）強烈

6 option [ˈɑpʃən] (n.) 選擇

7 inconceivable [͵ɪnkənˈsivəbl̩] (a.) 不能想像的；不可思議的

8 faith [feθ] (n.) 信念；信仰

And finally, I helped him, his thin arm round my neck, back to the steamer.

We left the next day at noon. The natives came running out of the woods again and filled the area below the house on the hill. Two thousand eyes watched the steamer. Three men covered in bright red mud, with horned heads, walked up and down in front of the crowd of people, stamping their feet and shaking black feathers at us. They shouted and the crowd chanted replies.

Kurtz watched from the couch[1] in my captain's cabin. Suddenly the woman with the helmet of hair ran to the very edge of the river. She put out her hands and shouted something, and everyone took up the shout in a roaring[2] chorus[3].

"Do you understand this?" I asked.

He kept looking out past me with fiery, longing eyes, with a mixed expression of wanting and hate.

"I certainly do," he said slowly, with a small, meaningful smile on his lips.

I pulled the string of the whistle, because I saw the agents from headquarters getting their guns out. At the sudden screech there was a movement of complete terror[4] amongst the huge crowd. I blew it again and again, and they ran away, twisting[5] and turning. The three men in red fell down on the bank, face down, as if they had been killed. Only the wild and proud woman did not move, stretching her arms after us over the shining river.

The brown current ran out of the heart of darkness, carrying us down towards the sea with twice the speed of our upward progress; and Kurtz's life was running swiftly, too, flowing out of his heart into the sea of time. The manager was very quiet; he felt that things had ended as he wanted.

Kurtz talked. A voice! A voice! It rang deep to the very end. His brain was full of shadowy images now—images of wealth and fame. He spoke of "my Intended, my station, my career, my ideas'.

The steamer broke down—as I had expected—and we had to wait for repairs by a small island. This delay shook Kurtz's confidence[6].

One morning he gave me a packet of papers and a photograph tied together with a shoelace[7].

"Keep this for me," he said. "This fool (meaning the manager) is capable of looking in my boxes when I am not there."

I didn't have much time for Kurtz just then because I was helping to repair the engine.

One evening when I came in with a candle I was surprised to hear him say: "I am lying here waiting for death."

"Oh, nonsense!" I replied.

---

1 couch [kautʃ] (n.) 臥榻
2 roaring [`rorɪŋ]
   (a.) 咆哮的；喧嘩的
3 chorus [`korəs] (n.) 合唱團
4 terror [`tɛrɚ] (n.) 恐怖；驚駭
5 twist [twɪst] (v.) 扭轉；轉身
6 confidence [`kɑnfədəns] (n.) 信心
7 shoelace [`ʃu,les] (n.) 鞋帶

His face changed, and I saw expressions of pride, power, terror—of an intense and hopeless despair[1].

Did he live his life again in that moment?

He cried out twice, a cry that was no more than a breath: "The horror! The horror!"

Chapter 7

I blew the candle out[2] and left the cabin. I went to join the colleagues from headquarters for dinner. Suddenly the manager's boy put his head round the door and said: "Mister Kurtz—he dead."

Everyone else rushed to see, while I went on with my dinner. However, I didn't eat much. There was a lamp in there and outside it was so terribly dark. I didn't go near the remarkable man again.

The next day the agents buried him in a muddy hole. The voice was gone. But I remained to dream the nightmare out to the end, and to show my loyalty[3] to Kurtz once more.

Destiny[4]. My destiny! He was a remarkable man. He had something to say. He had seen much, his stare was wide enough to take in the whole universe, and sharp enough to penetrate all the hearts that beat in the darkness.

He had summed it all up[5]—he had judged. "The horror!" His cry was an affirmation[6], a moral victory paid for by many defeats[7], by horrible fears, by terrible satisfactions. But it was a victory! That is why I have remained loyal to Kurtz to the last.

---

1 despair [dɪ'spɛr] (n.) 絕望
2 blow out 吹熄
3 loyalty ['lɔɪəltɪ] (n.) 忠誠
4 destiny ['dɛstənɪ] (n.) 命運；天命
5 sum it up 下總結
6 affirmation [ˌæfə'meʃən] (n.) 肯定；斷言
7 defeat [dɪ'fit] (n.) 失敗

Back in London, I found the daily life of ordinary people ridiculous, after what I had experienced. I kept the packet of papers given me by Kurtz, not knowing exactly what to do with it.

I was approached by a man from the company, who said they had the right to the papers. I gave him the report on the "Suppression of Savage Customs" to read, but after glancing at it, he said that was not what he had expected. He left, and I didn't see him again.

Someone who called himself Kurtz's cousin appeared two days later, and told me that Kurtz had essentially[1] been a great musician. I had never been able to decide what profession Kurtz had: a painter, a journalist[2]? But we both agreed that he was a universal[3] genius. I gave the old man some unimportant family letters and he left happily.

Finally a journalist came, asking to know something of the fate of his "dear colleague".

He told me he thought that Kurtz was not a good writer. "But heavens! How that man could talk. He electrified[4] large meetings. He had the faith, you see. He could get himself to believe anything. He would have been an excellent leader of an extreme political party[5]."

 "Which party?" I asked.

"Any party," answered the man. "He was an extremist, wasn't he?"

I agreed. I gave him the report to publish[6] if he felt it was worth it, and he left contented[7].

Kurtz

- Make a list of all the different things Kurtz could do.

So in the end I was left with a slim[8] packet of letters and the girl's portrait. I thought she had a beautiful expression. I decided I would go and give her the letters and portrait.

I felt that everything that had been Kurtz's had passed out of my hands: his soul, his body, his station, his ivory, his career. There remained only his memory and his Intended. So I went to see her.

As I walked to the house I had Kurtz before me, as usual. Visions of him on the stretcher, the wild crowd of adoring natives, the gloom of the forests, the river, and the beat of the drums, regular as a beating heart—the heart of a victorious darkness.

---

1 essentially [ɪˈsɛnʃəlɪ] (adv.) 本質上地
2 journalist [ˈdʒɝnəlɪst] (n.) 新聞記者
3 universal [ˌjunəˈvɝsl] (a.) 多才多藝的
4 electrify [ɪˈlɛktrəˌfaɪ] (v.) 使激動

5 political party 政黨
6 publish [ˈpʌblɪʃ] (v.) 出版
7 contented [kənˈtɛntɪd] (a.) 滿足的
8 slim [slɪm] (a.) 微少的

46 And the memory of what I had heard him say went with me, too. I remembered his pleading[1], his threats[2], his huge desires, his meanness[3], and the pain in his soul. As I rang the bell of the door, he seemed to stare out of it at me, that wide stare that accepted and hated all the universe. I seemed to hear his whispered cry: "The horror! The horror!"

I waited in a large sitting room with three long windows from floor to ceiling. There was a tall, cold marble[4] fireplace and a massive grand piano in the corner. A high door opened and closed. I stood up.

She came forward, all in black, with a pale head. She was in mourning[5].

It was more than a year since his death, but she seemed as if she wanted to remember and mourn forever. Her eyes looked out at me with great depth, confidence and trustfulness. But as we shook hands, I saw an expression of great desolation[6] come upon her face. For her, he had only died this minute.

We sat down and I laid the packet gently on a little table.

She put her hand over it. "You knew him well," she murmured.

"Intimacy[7] grows quickly out there," I said. "I knew him as well as it is possible for one man to know another."

"And you admired him," she said. "It was impossible to know him and not to admire him."

---

1 pleading [ˈplidɪŋ] (n.) 懇求
2 threat [θrɛt] (n.) 威脅
3 meanness [ˈminəs] (n.) 惡意的行為
4 marble [ˈmɑrbl̩] (a.) 大理石的
5 mourning [ˈmornɪŋ] (n.) 悲傷
6 desolation [ˌdɛsl̩ˈeʃən] (n.) 悲涼
7 intimacy [ˈɪntəməsɪ] (n.) 親密

"He was a remarkable man," I replied. "It was impossible not to . . ."

"Love him," she finished quickly, silencing me. "How true! But no one knew him so well as I! I knew him best."

The room was growing darker, but her forehead, smooth and white, remained illuminated[1] by her eternal[2] light of belief and love.

"You were his friend," she went on. "You must have been if he gave you this and sent you to me. I feel I can speak to you. Oh, I must speak to you. I want you—you who heard his last words— to know I have been worthy of[3] him."

I listened. It grew darker. She talked as thirsty men drink.

"Who was not his friend who heard him speak?" she continued. "He was able to bring out the best in people that he met. It is the gift of great men. But you have heard him! You know!"

"Yes, I know," I said

"What a loss to me—to us—to the world." I could see her eyes were full of tears that would not fall. "I have been very happy— very fortunate—very proud," she went on. "Too fortunate. Too happy for a little while. And now I am unhappy—for life. And all of his promise, his greatness, his generous mind, his noble heart, nothing remains—nothing but a memory. You and I—"

"We shall always remember him," I said quickly.

Admiration

- Why do you think Kurtz was loved and admired by so many different people and for so many different reasons?

"And his words will remain," she said. "And his example. Men looked up to him—his goodness shone in every act he did. I cannot believe that I shall never see him again, that nobody will see him again, never, never, never."

She put out her arms as if somebody were leaving. Never see him! I saw him clearly enough then. I shall see his eloquent phantom[4] as long as I live.

"You were with him—to the last?"

"To the very end," I said, shakily. "I heard his very last words . . ." I stopped in fright[5].

"Repeat them," she murmured in a heart-broken tone. "I want something to live with."

It was getting dark now and the darkness seemed to be repeating, "The horror! The horror!"

"His last words. To live with," she insisted. "Don't you understand I loved him—I loved him!"

I concentrated and spoke slowly. "The last word he pronounced was—your name."

---

1 illuminate [ɪˈlumə,net] 3 worthy of 配得上的
　(v.) 照亮；使容光煥發 4 phantom [ˈfæntəm] (n.) 幽靈；鬼魂
2 eternal [ɪˈtɝnl] (a.) 永恆的 5 fright [fraɪt] (n.) 驚嚇

I heard a short sigh. Then there was a loud and terrible cry of unbelievable triumph[1] and terrible pain.

"I knew it," she said. "I was sure!"

She knew. She was sure. She hid her face in her hands and wept[2].

Kurtz always said he wanted justice. But I couldn't. I couldn't tell her the truth. It would have been too dark, too dark—too dark altogether.

With these words Marlow finished his story.

He sat apart and silent. Nobody on board the *Nellie* moved for a time. The sky was dark and the river was black, seeming to lead into the heart of an immense darkness.

1 triumph ['traɪəmf] (n.) 勝利
2 weep [wip] (v.) 哭泣
   （三態：weep; wept; wept）

AFTER READING

Ⓐ Personal Response

1 Which elements of a "good story" (see page 19) do you think
Heart of Darkness has? Tick (✓).

    ⓐ Background and description.

    ⓑ Good plot with lots of action.

    ⓒ Satisfactory ending.

    ⓓ Hidden meaning and moral.

    ⓔ Convincing characters.

2 Did you enjoy the story? Why/Why not?

3 This is what some critics have said about *Heart of Darkness:*

    ⓐ ". . . a psychological masterpiece."

    ⓑ "Conrad's novel is also relevant today as modern man
is often displaced by war, famine and genocide."

    ⓒ "Conrad was a racist."

    ⓓ ". . . a dream of self-discovery."

Which comments do you agree with?
Which do you disagree with? Give reasons.

ⓑ Comprehension

4 Tick (✓) true (T) or false (F). Correct the false sentences.

T F   ⓐ Marlow is in France when he begins to tell his story.

T F   ⓑ Marlow's new job for a trading company takes him to Africa.

T F   ⓒ His first impressions of Africa are negative.

T F   ⓓ He is in Africa to bring back sugar.

T F   ⓔ He hears many stories about a man named Kurtz.

T F   ⓕ Nobody seems to like Kurtz.

T F   ⓖ Meeting Kurtz becomes Marlow's main goal.

T F   ⓗ In the end Kurtz leaves the jungle with Marlow.

5 Complete the sentences with the words and expressions from the box.

| admired | girlfriend | broke down |
| ill | journalist | papers |

ⓐ Marlow's steamer _____ at the beginning and at the end of his journey on the river.

ⓑ Marlow met a lot of people on his expedition but only _____ Kurtz.

ⓒ Kurtz was very _____ when Marlow finally met him.

ⓓ Kurtz was said to have many careers. He was even a _____.

ⓔ Before dying Kurtz gave Marlow a photograph and some _____.

ⓕ Marlow took a packet of things to Kurtz's _____.

6 Put these scenes from the story in chronological order.

7 Write a couple of sentences to describe each scene in Exercise **6**.

Include: the place, the people, what's happening, etc.

8 Who says these things? Match the sentences with the character.

(Marlow)   (the accountant)

(Kurtz)   (Kurtz's girlfriend)

_____ a "The horror! The horror!"

_____ b "Oh, Kurtz will go very far…he will become important in the administration before long."

_____ c "What a loss to me—to us—to the world!"

_____ d "I think Kurtz is a remarkable man."

9 Put the quotations in context. When were these things said? To whom?

a

b

c

d

81

C Characters

10 Complete the sentences about Marlow and Kurtz with the words from the box.

adventure	dark	loyal	trading
sent	sail	natives	Africa

a He liked _____ and was attracted to _____.

b He saw it first as a map of a big _____ area near the equator with a huge river in its center.

c He got a job for a _____ company and had to _____ down the Congo River.

d He was _____ to bring back Kurtz.

e His journey was difficult and his boat was even attacked by _____.

f He remained _____ to Kurtz to the last.

tribe	respected	mystery	focus

g There is a lot of _____ surrounding his character.

h Marlow's meeting with him soon becomes the main _____ of the story.

i Marlow understands that Kurtz is _____ by everyone.

j When Marlow finally meets him he sees he is living with a _____.

11 Kurtz is a contradictory character. Read these sentences and discuss the following in groups.

(a) Do you think Kurtz was helping the African people or using them?

(b) Was Kurtz a hero or a madman?

Each station must be like a light on the road to better things. A center for trade, of course, but also for improving the natives and instructing them.

The only way to stop the traditions was to exterminate all the natives.

Kurtz says:

Marlow says about Kurtz:

Kurtz's soul was mad. Being alone in the wilderness . . . it had gone mad.

It had become my job not to betray Kurtz. I have remained loyal to Kurtz to the last.

12 Go back to page 4. How was Marlow similar to Conrad?

D Plot and Theme

13 The story looks at the theme of the "colonizer or exploiter."
Match a sentence with its corresponding quote.

☐1 The Romans first came to London . . . they were
conquerors. They just took what they could get.

☐2 Going out to Africa to help those ignorant millions
change their horrible ways and bring them civilization.

☐3 Conquest is not a nice thing when you look at it too
closely: it is robbery and murder on a large scale.

_____ a The people in Africa need to be educated.

_____ b Stealing the land from those who are different to us.

_____ c England was also once colonized.

14 What view does Conrad give of Africa and the colonizer?
Find examples in the story and fill in the table below.

VIEW OF AFRICA

VIEW OF THE COLONIZER

15 Kurtz's last words, and the most famous words of the novel are "The horror! The horror!" In groups of four discuss what you think Kurtz was referring to.

16 Another theme in the story is that of the journey and how it can change us. Answer the following questions.

    a What is the exact journey that Marlow goes on?

    b What did Marlow see in Africa that changed him?

    c How was Kurtz changed by Africa? How was he living when Marlow found him?

17 The narrator is the person who tells the story. Who are the narrators in *Heart of Darkness*? Tick (✓).

    a Marlow.

    b Marlow and Kurtz.

    c One of the friends on the *Nellie* and Marlow.

    d Kurtz and one of the friends on the *Nellie*.

18 Conrad uses a frame narrative for Marlow to tell his story. This means it is a story within a story and it begins and ends on the boat, the *Nellie*, in London. What effect does this have on the reader? Tick (✓).

    a It makes the reader feel he/she has been on a journey.

    b It makes the story seem longer.

    c It makes Africa seem very far.

E Language

19 Complete the sentences with one of the two words "dark" and "darkness".

[a] The air was _____, and there was a great gloom all over the city.

[b] It was a map of a big _____ area near the equator with a huge river in its center.

[c] The _____ green jungle was almost black beside the glittering sea.

[d] For me we were crawling towards Kurtz—exclusively, as we penetrated further and further into the heart of _____.

[e] What powers of _____ had taken him?

[f] The brown current ran out of the heart of _____, carrying us down towards the sea with twice the speed of our upward progress.

20 Darkness is the strongest symbol in the story.

> **symbol:** something that represents or stands for something else, usually by association

What do you think darkness symbolizes in *Heart of Darkness*? Choose.

_____ [a] the jungle   _____ [d] Africa

_____ [b] the negative side of   _____ [e] aspects of colonization
man's character

[c] the natives   _____ [f] night

21 Our daily lives are full of symbols. Look at the following symbols and write below each one what they represent.

> escalator   turn on/off   nuclear energy
> power   the weather   interconnection

a _____

b _____

c _____

d _____

e _____

f _____

22 The story takes place on a river. Use these words to complete the sentences below.

> up river   anchored   down river   bank   current

a We were sitting on the *Nellie*; a sailing boat.
We were _____ in the Thames in London.

b It's difficult and dangerous to swim in this river as the
_____ is so strong.

c I believed that the jungle on either _____
was impenetrable.

d We left the port and sailed _____ as we wanted
to see the countryside.

e If we keep on travelling _____ we'll soon reach
the sea.

TEST

1 Listen and tick (✓) the correct picture.

a **1**  **2**

b **1**  **2**

c **1**  **2**

d **1**  **2**

P **2** Choose the correct answer.

_____ a The main story is told by _____.

    ① Kurtz   ③ Marlow

    ② the accountant   ④ Kurtz's girlfriend

_____ b Who helped Marlow get his job with the trading company?

    ① His girlfriend.   ③ His aunt.

    ② Kurtz.   ④ The owner of the company.

_____ c What position is he given in the company?

    ① Accountant.   ③ Sailor.

    ② Mechanic.   ④ Captain.

_____ d Marlow's adventure takes place on _____.

    ① the Congo River   ③ the Amazon River

    ② the Thames   ④ the Nile

_____ e Marlow's first impression of Africa is _____.

    ① negative   ③ positive

    ② confused   ④ idealized

_____ f What does his company bring back from Africa?

    ① Gold.   ③ Sugar.

    ② Tobacco.   ④ Ivory.

_____ ⓖ What is unusual about the crew of
Marlow's boat?
① They are Russian.
② They are French.
③ They can't speak English.
④ They are all cannibals.

_____ ⓗ Who is the most successful trader in
the company?
① Kurtz. ③ The Russian.
② The owner. ④ Marlow.

_____ ⓘ Why is Marlow told to bring Kurtz back?
① Because he's dangerous.
② Because he's mad.
③ Because he's ill.
④ Because he's a criminal.

_____ ⓙ What do the natives think about Kurtz?
① They think he's a god.
② They don't like him.
③ They are afraid of him.
④ They are indifferent.

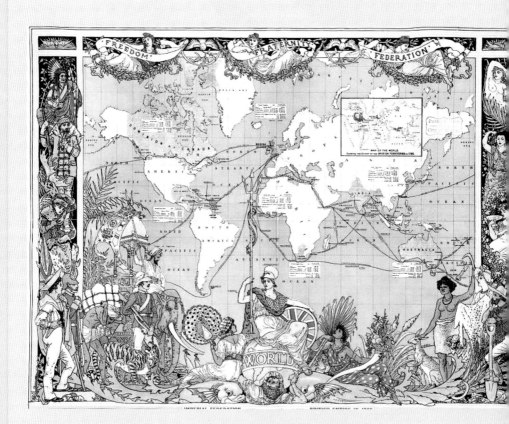

[Web] **1** Here is an image of the British Empire when Conrad wrote *Heart of Darkness*. Do some research and find out which countries were governed by Britain; when the Empire ended; who was king/queen during this period.

2 Interview with Marlow. Marlow has just returned from Africa. You have been asked by your local newspaper to interview him. Prepare some questions using:

When?   Who?   What?
Where?   Why?   How?

Work with a partner and take it in turns to ask and answer each other's questions.

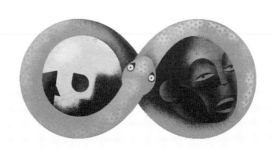

作者簡介

1857 年，約瑟夫‧康拉德（Joseph Conrad）出生於波蘭的別爾基切夫（Berdychiv），本名 Jozef Teodor Konrad Nalecz Korzeniowski。童年時期，康拉德住在烏克蘭和俄國，雙親過世後，由在波蘭的叔叔照顧長大成人。

康拉德自小學習法文，閱讀莎士比亞的作品，很喜愛波蘭浪漫詩人的作品，也熱愛海洋。他一畢業，叔叔就讓他出海。 1878 年，他加入英國商船隊，而且最後當上了船長。

康拉德航遍全世界， 1890 年，他來到比屬剛果，這是他日後的作品《黑暗之心》（1902）的靈感來源。然而，這一趟航行也讓他罹病。到了 1894 年，主要由於健康問題，他放棄航海，成為全職作家。

1886 年，康拉德入英國國籍。他離開船隊後，定居於英國南部。 1895 年，他的第一部小說《奧邁耶的癡夢》（Almayer's Folly）問世，講述在婆羅洲海岸的一場探險故事。 1896 年，他和潔西‧喬治（Jessie George）結婚，育有兩子。他雖然定期出版短篇故事、小說和散文，但一直到 1913 年出版的《機緣》（Chance）大受歡迎之後，財務狀況才得以好轉。

在作家的眼中，康拉德被公認是一位傑出的作者，他的小說《吉姆老爺》（Lord Jim, 1900）、《黑暗之心》（1902）、《諾斯楚摩》（Nostromo, 1904）、《密探》（The Secret Agent, 1907）、《在西方的眼界下》（Under Western Eyes, 1911），頗受好評。雖然英文是他的第三語言，但是他對英文的掌握能力、運筆風格，令人印象深刻。 1924 年，康拉德因心臟病過世。

本書簡介 就像約瑟夫·康拉德的許多小說一樣,《黑暗之心》也是根據他的行船經驗所寫成的。故事和他在剛果河一艘汽船上擔任船長的一段經歷有關,當時他為比利時一家貿易公司效勞。後來他因病返鄉,並對比利時人對當地人民的帝國主義態度感到極度失望。

《黑暗之心》的故事中有兩位敘事者,一位是聶力號(Nellie)上的匿名者,另一位是馬洛(Marlow)。第一位敘事者為整本小說起了頭,隨後介紹馬洛出場,接著由馬洛來講述自己的經歷。在馬洛講完自己的故事之後,再交回給匿名敘事者,講述故事的尾聲。像這樣的敘事方式,稱為框架敘事法(frame narrative)。

《黑暗之心》的主要故事,由船員馬洛所講述出來。他跟其他船員講他在非洲一條大河上擔任汽船船長時的經歷。馬洛的工作是運送象牙,然後把公司最優秀的象牙代理商庫爾茲(Kurtz)先生帶回來,當時庫爾茲已經病重。

他們的船隻因為維修,啟程延誤許久,爾後沿河而上。他們找到了庫爾茲,而庫爾茲當時儼然已經成了當地人的首領。最後,馬洛將他帶上船,但庫爾茲卻在河中回航時,病逝於船上。

書名中的「黑暗」兩個字,在故事中象徵了多重意思,包括叢林、邪惡、貪腐、剝削。而到最後,庫爾茲先生似乎是選擇黑暗,而不是將光明帶給人們。

這本小說抨擊了殖民主義和帝國主義,但康拉德被批評在書中抹滅非洲人的人性,僅將他們視為是危險暗叢中的一部份。

《黑暗之心》被翻譯為多種語言,也被改編為廣播劇和電視劇,而其中最著名的改編版本,就是法蘭西斯·柯波拉(Francis Ford Coppola)的電影《現代啟示錄》(Apocalypse, 1979)。

第一章

P. 17

夜幕降臨，我們坐在一艘帆船聶力號上。我們停泊在倫敦的泰晤士河，等待潮汐轉向，以便啟程。天色黑漆漆的，整座城市籠罩在一片深沉的黑暗中。我們五個人都是經驗老道的船員，而且大家都是老朋友了，聚在一起很放鬆。黑幕愈轉愈深，眼前穿梭兩岸的舟火，愈來愈多。

「這裡也算得上是世界上最黑暗的地方了。」馬洛突然開口說道。

在我們這幾個人當中，只有馬洛還是在役船員。他是海員，也喜歡浪蕩天涯。不管是船隻、海洋，還是他到過的異域碼頭、見過的異國臉孔，都讓他感到興味盎然。那些他到過的地方、遇到過的人，愈是難解，他就愈是興致勃勃，想一探究竟。所以啦，他說什麼，都不會讓我們吃驚，我們也不會提出異議。接著，他緩緩地繼續道來。

P. 18

「我想到古老以前，羅馬人第一次踏上這塊土地，那是一千九百年以前的事啦。他們沿著泰晤士河，一路航行到黑暗荒涼的地方，當時天候惡劣，伙食不佳，死亡四伏。不過，羅馬人夠強悍的了，有能耐面對眼前這一片黑暗。他們是征服者，能掠奪什麼就掠奪什麼。

征服，可不是一件什麼美好的事，仔細研究一下，是大規模的燒殺擄掠呀。不過當然啦，征服者會把征服看成是一個什麼高尚之舉，具有什麼真正的意義。」

馬洛停下來。我們看著河上的燈火，耐心地等他繼續說下去。好一陣靜默之後，馬洛繼續說道：「我航行過一條大河。」我們知道，他要跟我們說的是他一段結果並不圓滿的漫長經歷。

馬洛開始了他的故事。

我不想拿太多我個人的經歷來叨擾諸位，不過為了讓你們明白這趟航行對我所造成的影響，有些事情得先讓你們知道：我是怎麼到那裡的？我看到了什麼？我又是怎麼沿著河，來到我第一次遇到庫爾茲的地方？

P.19

一個好的故事

• 對你來說,在一個故事中,以下哪些元素是重要的?請打勾。
 □ 背景和敘述內容。
 □ 劇情精彩,有很多動作場景。
 □ 圓滿的結局。
 □ 隱藏的意涵和寓意。
 □ 具說服力的人物角色。

在找下一份工作前,我在倫敦四處閒晃休息。原本,我是打算回海上,但是找不到船家。後來有一天,我在商店櫥窗看到了小時候看過的一張地圖,那是赤道附近一塊很大的黑暗區域,中心地帶橫亙著一條大河流。我拿定主意,就要去那個地方:非洲。

我記得有家外國公司就在剛果河流域進行買賣交易,而我有個姑姑剛好認識那家公司的其中一位老闆。多虧了姑姑,我得到了那家公司的工作,成了一艘河上汽船的船長。

P.21

就在四十八小時內,我越過英吉利海峽,去見在比利時的老闆,簽了合約。當我在那裡時,他們要求我要做健康檢查,一位老醫生量了我的脈搏,還量了我的頭圍。我覺得很奇怪,就問他這有什麼好量的。

「那些去非洲的人,他們會面臨的最大改變,就發生在他們的腦袋裡。」他神祕兮兮地說。

接著,他問我,家族裡有沒有人發瘋的病史,這可激怒我了,我也直接跟他說他的問題讓我很火大。

「只要記得,你去非洲之後,不要火大就好。在熱帶地區,憤怒比太陽還危險。保持冷靜,沉著點。再見了。」他在揮手示意要我離開前說道。

上工前,我前去謝謝姑姑。她對我很好,而且好像把我當成是某種「光明使者」,要去非洲幫助「上百萬無知的人,改變他們駭人的生活方式,為他們帶來文明」。

不過我提醒她,我是要去為一家只對賺錢有興趣的公司幹活而已。

我覺得自己要去的地方,不是某塊大陸的中心,而是世界的中心。

P.22

佔領與殖民

• 馬洛要去哪裡?
• 他現在工作的公司隸屬於哪個國家?
• 馬洛提到了羅馬對英國的佔領,在字典裡查一下 conquest 這個字的意思。馬洛決定為一家在非洲進行買賣貿易的歐洲公司工作,你對歐洲在非洲殖民的狀況瞭解有多少?在字典裡查一下 colonization 這個字的意思。
• 佔領與殖民有什麼不同?請小組討論。

第二章

P.23

我搭了一艘法國汽船離開。我們沿著非洲海岸航行，沿岸看似是一片荒野的外緣。深綠色的叢林在閃閃發光的海洋旁，幾乎是一片黑暗。我們偶爾會看到划著船的黑皮膚人，能看到他們，是一種很大的安慰，能夠短暫地接觸到現實世界。有一回，我們碰上一艘停泊在海岸外的法國船隻，他們無故地對叢林重槍開火。

在我們抵達大河的河口前，已經度過了三十多天。後來，我換了船，和一位瑞典籍的年輕船長搭上一艘較小的汽船，往上游駛去。他告訴我，他最近帶了另一名瑞典籍的船員沿河而上，但那名船員半途中自殺了。

我問他是什麼原因，他回答：「誰知道！搞不好是受不了這裡的大太陽，或是受不了這個地方。」

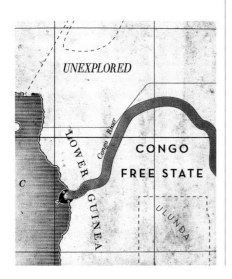

最後，我們抵達一個土壤都被翻挖過的地方。那裡有很多人，大多是黑人，他們穿著動物的毛皮，像螞蟻一樣四處遊走。在一座山坡上，房子林立，還有一個延伸入河的碼頭。

「那就是你們公司的駐所。」瑞典籍船長指著岩石山上的三棟木頭建築，説道：「我會把你的東西送上去。再見！」

P.24

我走上通往駐所的步道。黑人工人正在造鐵路，到處都是壞掉的機械和生鏽的鐵軌。時不時，那些土著就跑去找掩護，然後是一陣爆炸震動了大地。彷彿在進行中的工作中，只有這些爆炸是上軌道的。

樹蔭下，我看到躺著黑色的身影。我很快發現，他們是來躲太陽的工人，如今已經筋疲力竭到在這裡等死。他們神情茫然，眼神空洞，躺的姿勢很不自然。我停住，驚恐地看著他們，然後快步離開，往駐所前去。

快走到建築物時，我見到了一個白人，後來我才知道他是公司的會計主任。他看起來像幻影一樣，一身白衣，純淨無瑕。他穿著乾淨的襯衫，打著領帶，穿著夾克和白色的長褲，一雙靴子擦得發亮，一頭分邊的頭髮梳得整整齊齊的。我和他握了手。

那位會計先生和他的帳簿都很整齊。他來這裡三年了，他已經訓練了一位土著女士來照顧他和他的衣服。

但除此之外，一切都是一團糟——包括人啦、東西啦、建築物啦。許多土著來了又走，他們帶著劣質的棉花球串和銅線，走進叢林的深處，深入河域，然後帶著一小支珍貴的象牙回到駐所，當作交換。

P. 25

貿易

• 這家公司買賣什麼東西？在哪裡買賣？
• 這種產品和交易，你有所瞭解嗎？請小組討論。

我得在這外圍的交易站待上十天，感覺像永無止盡的漫長。我會在會計先生那悶熱的木造辦公室裡待些時候，在這裡，他就坐在書桌前的高凳子上寫著數字。他就是第一個跟我提到庫爾茲的人。

有一天，他頭也沒抬地開口說了：「你在內陸，一定會碰到庫爾茲。」

一問之下，我才知道庫爾茲是一流的仲介商，很出色。在真正象牙的國度裡，他負責一個很重要的交易站。他獲取的象牙量，可抵所有其他仲介商的總合。

P. 27

他繼續說：「你碰到庫爾茲時，幫我跟他說，這裡一切盡如人意。我不喜歡寫信給他，因為你永遠不知道在中央駐所裡，收到信的可能會是誰。」他停了一下，看了我一會兒，又繼續說：「喔，庫爾茲不可限量，沒多久，他會在管理部門擔任要角，就是歐洲那些老大們，想要拉拔他。」

職涯

• 為什麼會計先生認為庫爾茲的前途不可限量？
• 「不可限量」對你來說是什麼意思？跟朋友分享你的看法。

隔天，我和六十人的商隊離開駐所。每個人都為三百英哩的路程帶了大量的物資。

我們走過縱橫交錯的小道，穿越草原長路、燒毀的草叢、灌木叢，在熾熱的高溫下，在滿佈石頭的山坡爬上爬下，後來來到一大片荒地。那裡的居民早都撤走了，我們踏過這個空無一人的村莊。

同行的人當中，有一個白人肥仔。一開始時，在高溫下，他不斷地昏厥過去，所以我得用我自己的外套幫他擋太陽。我忍不住問他為什麼要來這裡。

P. 28

「當然是為了賺錢。」他回答。

後來,他開始發燒,得要人背。不過,因為他的體重,背他的那些人起了爭執。

十五天後,我們抵達中央駐所。它位於大河中的一個死水區,被灌木叢和森林圍繞著。

另外一個白肥仔,就是幾個帶著長手杖來盤問我的其中一個仲介商,他告訴我,我的汽船在河底,並說我應該立刻去見總經理。很明顯地,有個自願幫忙的船長讓船撞上岩石,船底破洞了。汽船就沉在河的南岸,要把船從河裡拉上來修理好,要花上我好幾個月的時間。

那個經理看起來毫不起眼,有著一雙冷漠的藍眼睛。大家都聽他的,但不是出於喜愛、畏懼或尊敬,而是因為他在這裡所獲取到的權力。他是個很平凡的生意人,三年來努力管好自己的健康。在這裡,這是很少見的。他不擅於組織,沒有進取心,也沒有條理。這是顯而易見的,因為駐所搞得一塌糊塗。他也沒有什麼學識才智,只是讓一切按部就班的運作。

也不管我已經走了三十英哩,那位經理早上一看到我,就開始跟我陳述狀況。上游駐所的人要撤換,他們已經延誤很多次了;他們不知道誰死了、誰還活著,也不知道他們的狀況如何;他如此這般地跟我講了很多。還有謠言說,有個重要的駐所岌岌可危,因為那裡的頭頭庫爾茲病了。他憂心忡忡,問那艘船要花多久時間才能修好。

P. 29

「我怎麼知道?我連船都還沒看到,大概要幾個月吧。」我說。

「那我們就算三個月好了,這時間應該夠了吧,然後你就可以去庫爾茲那裡了。」他說。

我走出他的小屋,自言自語地喃喃唸著他這個人是個白痴。不過,後來那艘船的修理時間真的是三個月不差時,我收回了這句話。

隔天,我走到河邊去看那艘船。我回頭看駐所,看到公司的仲介商們拿著可笑的長手杖,在太陽下閒晃著。空中迴響著「象牙」這兩個字,那是呢喃輕嘆聲,猶如那些仲介商正在禱告一樣。我這輩子沒有目睹過這麼虛幻不實的場景,唯一的現實,大概就是他們巴望著能被派到可以找到象牙的交易站,這樣才有利可圖。

而四周圍,包圍這些活動的寂靜荒野,偉然無敵,似邪似正,靜待這場掠奪消失無蹤。

P. 30

幾天後,我碰到一個做磚塊的人,儘管他已經沒有原料可以做磚了。也因為這樣,他跟其他仲介商一樣無所事事。他邀我到他屋裡聊聊。我看到牆上有一幅女人的畫,他說那是庫爾茲在一年多前畫的。

「請跟我說這個庫爾茲到底是誰?」我說。

P. 31

「他是內陸駐所的頭頭,一個奇才。今

天，他是第一流駐所的頭頭；明年，他就會是副理，再個過兩年可就……。我想你應該知道他日後的來頭。你是新團隊的一員，就是派他來的那些人，推薦你來的，這我知道。」他回答。

他所說的，和事實大相逕庭，讓我差點笑出來。我姑姑那些有權有勢的朋友，對其他人起了一些奇怪的影響力。

我的工作需要鉚釘。他們在沿海地區有好幾箱鉚釘，但是我們這裡什麼都沒有。我們有鐵板可以用在修補上，卻沒有東西可以把鐵板鎖緊，所以我沒辦法繼續我的工作，去把船上的洞補起來。

在等待的期間，我有很多時間來好好想想庫爾茲這個人。我對他個人並不特別感興趣，不過我好奇這種帶著某種道德理想來到這裡的人，最後是不是能攀上最高的地位，而到時候，他又要如何推動他的工作。

駐所

• 你有留意到各個駐所的不同名字嗎？

第三章

P.32

有一晚，我平躺在汽船上的甲板，無意中聽到經理和一位同事談到庫爾茲的事。

我得知，庫爾茲要求可以到某個駐所去，好向管理部門展現他的能力。他帶著助理和象牙，沿河走了三百英哩，來到總部，但之後隨即返回自己的駐所，表示自己比較喜歡孤軍作戰。

我無意間聽到談話的這兩個人，都很驚訝怎麼會有人是如此行徑。我第一次覺得自己真的可以琢磨庫爾茲這個人了。一個隻身的白人，不理會庫爾茲總部和同事，帶著四個土著，划著獨木舟，回到自己在荒野中那個空蕩蕩、沒有人煙的駐所。

助理告訴經理，庫爾茲病得很重，只稍稍恢復了些。從那之後，似乎就沒什麼其他的消息了。這是九個月之前的事情。而象牙也從那之後就沒貨了。

「這又不是我的錯。」經理在這時插上了一句。

「這很讓人難過啊。」肥仔同事說。

P.33

「還有，他在這裡的時候，也很棘手。他講話就像這樣：『每一個駐所，都應該要像路上的燈，讓事情更美好。駐所當然是用來交易買賣，但也該用來讓土著變得更好，還要教導他們才對。』想想看，他根本就是自己想當經理嘛！」

不久之後，和我一起前來的肥仔仲介商離開了總部，他帶著他的團隊進入荒

野，後來我們就沒有他們的消息了。

我們也要離開了，前往庫爾茲的駐所。想到可以一睹庫爾茲的盧山真面目，這讓我很亢奮，儘管從我們離開總部，到抵達庫爾茲駐所下方的河岸，整整要花上兩個月的時間。

期待

- 你認為，為什麼要見到庫爾茲，會讓馬洛很興奮？
- 是否有久聞大名的人，讓你很想一睹盧山真面目？

P.35

尋河而上，那情景彷彿是在回溯世界誕生之初一樣，大地上四周都是植物，巨樹就是世界之王。空蕩蕩的河流，一大片的寂然，無法穿越的森林，空氣溫熱、濃稠而沉重，閃爍的陽光並沒有帶來愉悅。河水像被遺棄般，向陰暗的遠處流去。在一處銀色的沙洲上，浮著相鄰點點的河馬和鱷魚。一連串的小島，常把河流分割開來，讓人分不清主航道是哪一條。我一直注意著，生怕船底撞上了藏在水面下的岸頭。

然而，我們還是不斷地在修理壞掉的蒸汽管。我忙到常常忘了自己身在何處，但我覺得好像哪兒都一樣，那神祕的寂靜一直在盯著我看。

除了經理，我船上還有三、四個總部來的白人仲介商，以及二十個左右的食人族船員，當水位太淺無法航行時，他們常常得跳下船，幫忙拉推船身。我們還有一個火伕，他是一個土著，接受過觀察水位的訓練。他知道水位如果太低，鍋爐可能會爆炸，所以他戰戰兢兢地留意著船身的吃水深度。

P.36

有時，我們路過小駐所，會有一些白人衝出來，很興奮、很驚喜地歡迎我們。然後在我們繼續進入一片沉寂之前，「象牙」兩個字又在空中響起。

空蕩的水域，樹，都是樹，數百萬棵的樹，數不清，又高又大，小汽船就在當中緩緩地前進，令人感到渺小而失落。

不知道其他人想像中的目的地是如

何,大概是到可以搬回什麼東西的某個地方吧,我猜。而對我來說,隨著愈來愈進入黑暗之心的深處,我們就只是愈朝著庫爾茲接近。

遠征
• 汽船上有誰?他們要去哪裡?

四周很安靜,但在晚上,樹林中有時候會傳出鼓聲。那聲音彷彿在我們頭頂的上空縈繞著,一直到第一道曙光出現才消失。沒有人知道這些鼓聲代表著戰爭、和平還是祈禱。

有時候,我們會看到土著的村落,乾蘆葦築牆的房子,有著尖尖的茅草屋頂。河岸上,黑黝黝的雙手雙腳會突然倏地移動,或是一陣拍手、一陣跺步,或是移動身體。他們叫吼、跳動、旋轉,做出可怕的表情。

P.38

我們一路經過這種難以理解的畫面,繼續航行。我們對這周遭的一切,全然不解,這離我們現代世界中的日常生活太遙遠。但儘管距離遙遠,他們的行為還是和我們有所聯繫，畢竟他們和我們一樣都是人類，都是以同樣的方式感受著快樂、悲傷、恐懼或憤怒。

人類

- 你喜歡安靜還是熱鬧？
- 你喜歡靜態還是動態？

在內陸駐所下游處大約五十哩的地方，我們發現了一間蘆葦小屋，屋頂上插著旗竿，還有一疊整齊的裁切木頭。這讓我們感到意外。我將船開近河岸。在那疊木柴上寫著：「給你的木頭。趕快。謹慎地接近。」

我們不瞭解這話的意思。我們是要「趕快」去哪裡？往上游去嗎？開著這麼大聲的汽船，我們要怎麼「謹慎地接近」？河流的上游是出了什麼事？情況有多麼不妙呢？真是一團謎！

P.39

我們航行時，我原以為船隨時都可以停下來。不過，到了離開小屋後的第二天晚上，我們離庫爾茲的駐所只剩八英哩左右了。我想繼續前進，經理卻說溯河而上太危險了，最好等到早上再走。由於我們還有很多木材，所以我就將船停在河道中央，準備過夜。這是河道中平直的一段，兩旁有著高大的樹木。萬物寂然，接著夜幕降臨。

當太陽升起時，四周一片白霧，感覺像堅壁一樣。九點左右，霧很快散去了。短短幾分鐘內，我們又看到了河道、樹林和太陽。但接著霧又籠罩下來，隱沒了一切。

突然，寂靜被劃破，一個很大聲的叫喊聲響徹天空，接著是很多人一起叫囂不滿的聲音，再來又是一連串激動的喊叫，似乎一下子從四面八方傳來。不過，這些聲音突然響起，又突然止息。

總部的人拿著上膛的溫徹斯特來福槍，從船艙裡衝出來，但是上膛做什麼？眼前看到的只是我們自己身處的汽船，周遭一切都消失了。

104

第四章

P.41

我下令把鐵鏈拉起來，這樣等霧再散開時，就可以輕易地起錨，我們就能離開了。

「他們會攻擊嗎？」總部一個矮胖的男人，用驚恐的聲音小聲地說。

「這樣的霧，我們會被殺得一個不留。」另一個人回答。

食人族船員在拉鏈條時，食人族的頭頭就站在我旁邊。

「把他們抓起來！」他跟我說：「抓起來，然後交給我們。」

「交給你們？你們要怎麼處理？」我問。

「吃掉。」他看著霧回答。

當然，這我能瞭解。他和他的族人都餓了。他們只吃我們一個多月前出發時所帶的死河馬肉。我們沿途並沒有按計畫停靠岸邊，讓他去找更多的糧食。他們每個星期每個人可以拿到三段二十公分左右的黃銅絲，理論上他們可以用這種貨幣在河岸的村落購買糧食，但實際上卻行不通，因為不是沒有村莊，就是村民充滿敵意，或是經理因為個人的理由，不想停靠。

P.42

除了河馬肉，我唯一看到他們吃的，是一種用葉子包起來看起來像半熟麵包的東西。

既然我都能想到這一點了，我不知道這三十個人為什麼沒有把我們這五個白人宰了來吃。

食人族

• 你對食人族瞭解多少？上網研究一下，進行小組討論。

「這不是開玩笑的，在我們抵達之前，庫爾茲要是有個不測，那我就完了。」經理的聲音從我背後傳來。

儘管我躺在汽船甲板上時，聽過他說的一些話，但我相信他是說真的，他是那種想要保住面子的人。

「我們得立刻繼續前進。」他說。

我懶得回答他，因為我們都知道這根本就不可能。

「我授權由你負起所有的風險。」他在短暫的沉默後開口。

「我拒絕承擔任何風險。」我簡短地回答。

「好吧，我只得接受你的判斷，你是船長。」他用一種特別禮貌的方式說：「你想他們會攻擊嗎？」

P.43

基於幾個顯而易見的理由，我想他們不會發動攻擊。首先，是因為濃霧：這時搭獨木舟離開岸邊，他們也會迷失在霧中，這跟我們動彈不得的處境一樣。再者，兩岸的叢林非常茂密，我想是無法穿越的，儘管叢林裡藏了很多打量我們的眼睛。最後，在霧散開的那幾分鐘內，我沒有看到四周哪裡有獨木舟。

不過真正讓我覺得他們不會攻擊的原因，是因為他們所發出的聲音的特質：聲音傳達了強烈的悲傷。我們汽船的出現，不知怎麼地，讓這些人充滿了悲痛。

想想看

• 你認為，汽船的出現為什麼會讓土著悲傷？

終於，霧散了。我們沿河而上，來到距離庫爾茲的駐所約一英哩的地方，在那裡，河道上有一處得十分貼近河岸航行。河面上懸垂著一些樹和矮木叢。我從甲板上的船艙裡，仔細地看著一切。

P.44

船頭有個船員正在用桿子在測量水的深度。在我下方，火伕正把木材放進火爐裡。在我身旁，舵手正在操縱著船隻。突然間，船頭的船員倒在甲板上，火伕也蹲了下來。我嚇一大跳。

之後我往上一看，整個空中都是木枝，朝我們飛來。這整個過程，河流、河岸和樹林一直都很寂靜，所以我可以聽到引擎的聲音。然後突然間，箭雨紛落四處。箭！有人對我們大叫！

我快速走進船艙，拉上靠近陸地的百葉窗。葉叢間，我看到沉著凶猛的臉正盯著我看。我再仔細一瞧，看到林子裡藏滿了人。他們射出的箭飛向我們。在我下方的甲板上，總部的人拿著溫徹斯特來福槍衝出來，向樹叢開槍。隨著煙霧從槍口升起，整個場面一團混亂。

舵手抓住船艙裡的來福槍，拉開我拉上的百葉窗，往樹林裡掃射，但這是錯誤的舉動，因為有人在他的肋骨下方不知是射了還是推進了一支矛。他慢慢地滑下地板，痛苦地哀嚎著。

P.46

甲板上，槍枝傳來更多的射擊聲，還有叢林中人們失控的尖叫聲。我接手操控船隻，抓了汽笛，發出一連串尖銳刺耳的聲響。

森林中的喊叫聲停住了，接著是一長串恐懼悲痛的哀嚎，感覺像是人間的最後一絲希望已經破滅一樣。樹叢中，一陣人影晃動，箭雨倏然停住。

總部的一個仲介商帶著經理的口信過來，但我沒理他，反而要他操控船隻。

他看著躺在地板上的舵手。「他死了。」他靜靜地說。

「必然是死了。我猜，都這個關卡了，庫爾茲先生應該也死了吧。」我回答。

我感到極端的失望。在這場突擊之後，我很確定庫爾茲已經死了。我這才明白，我這樣一路過來，就是想聽他講話，但如今聽不到了。這不是因為他拿到的象牙，比所有其他仲介商加起來的還要多，關鍵是，他天賦異稟，而他最了不得的才華就是他的能言善道，說起話來像放光芒那樣。

我不禁想：「天啊，一切都結束了，我們太遲了。他死了，他的天賦消逝了。他被殺死了，我始終不可能聽到他講話了。」

P.47

不過，當然，我錯了。聽他講話的那份榮幸，還在等著我。是的，而且我聽得夠多了。

當我們來到庫爾茲的小屋時，我們看到了成疊的象牙。我們把象牙裝滿整艘汽船，連甲板上也堆了很多，這些都是庫爾茲的，所有的東西都是他的。

庫爾茲是這樣說的：「我的象牙，我的駐所，我的河流，我的未婚妻，我的……」這一切都是他的，不過我想知道的，那他自己是屬於誰的？是什麼黑暗力量把他帶走的？到底是什麼改變了他？顯然地，庫爾茲已經不是傳聞中所說的那個樣子。

庫爾茲在過世前，跟我說了很多事。

那是因為在和土著相處這麼久的時間之後，他很高興還能再講英文。他還給我看了一份他自己寫的報告〈壓制野蠻習俗〉，講述如何終止非洲土著的殘酷傳統。這份報告寫了十七頁。（我得說，他可以說是在發神經之前就寫好了這份報告，然後才開始參與那些會以最駭人的儀式作結尾的深夜舞蹈大會）。

P.48

讀這份報告時，他書寫的方式令我印象深刻，他言談流暢，用詞優雅，深富情感。然後，整個文章卻帶到了一個可怕的結論：要終止這些習俗的唯一方法，就是滅絕所有的土著。

他哀求我妥善保管他的這份報告。

黑暗的力量
• 你認為庫爾茲是哪裡出了問題？
• 你認為黑暗代表什麼？

這個故事我跳得太後面了。在突擊後，我們航行一小段，抵達了一個駐所。在那裡，我們碰上了一個白人，他穿著鮮艷補丁的衣服。他登上汽船。

「我可不喜歡這樣。叢林裡有土著。」我跟他說。

「他們都是頭腦簡單的人。」他說：「我很高興你們來了。我所有的時間都用在讓他們不要靠近。」

接著他開始快語地大談船隻和這些人，一副他好像很久沒和人說過話一樣。

P.50

「你沒有和庫爾茲談嗎?」我問。

「你沒有辦法跟他談什麼,你只有聽他說的份。」他回答。

接著我請他介紹自己。他是個俄國船員,是一家荷蘭貿易公司派他來叢林的。他解釋道,我們之前在樹林中看到的那間房子,原本是他的。

「要讓這些人離遠一點,很麻煩。」他說。

「他們想殺你嗎?」我問

「喔,不是。」他大叫。

「那他們為什麼攻擊我們?」我繼續問。

「他們不想讓庫爾茲離開。」他停了一下,回答道。

「他們不想?」我好奇地說。

他神祕地點點頭。「我告訴你,這個人讓我大開眼界。」他一邊說,一邊張開雙臂。

第五章

P.51

我看著這個一身色彩繽紛的俄國人,納悶他是如何生存下來的,如何一路大老遠沿河來到這個地方,還有他是怎麼想辦法讓自己留在這裡的。

「我一次走一點,愈走愈遠,直到我不知道該怎麼走回頭。沒關係,有的是時間,我可以處理的。我跟你說,你快帶庫爾茲走,快!」他說。

他告訴我他跟庫爾茲在一起的時光。我想庫爾茲很需要一個聽眾,因為有一回,他們一起在林子裡紮營時,聊了一整晚,而且可能大都是庫爾茲在講話。

「我們天南地北地聊。」他說。回憶讓他激動。「我都忘了還有睡覺這回事。我們無所不聊,也聊了個人的感情。他讓我懂了很多。」

「你從那時候開始,就跟著他了?」我問。

「不是。他喜歡一個人漫步,他常會深入森林。」他回答。

「他是去探險?」我問。

他告訴我,庫爾茲發現了很多村落,還有一座湖,但他不是很確定湖是位在哪個方向。不過,庫爾茲的探勘都還是為了象牙。

P.52

「老實說,他打劫了那些地方。」我暗示性地說。

他點點頭。

「當然,他不是單獨去的吧?他找到一個部落的人跟著他,是吧?」我問。

「他們崇拜他。」他説。

從他説這句話的樣子，就可以看出來庫爾茲已經占滿他的生活，霸佔了他的思想，左右他的情緒。

「你還能期待什麼？」他大吼著説：「他帶著雷電——他的槍，接近他們。他們沒有看過像那樣的東西。庫爾茲有可能變得可怕的，你不能像評斷一般人那樣來評斷他，絕對不行！他曾説過，如果我不給他象牙，他就會對我開槍。只要他高興，沒有什麼可以阻止他。而這也是事實。我給了他象牙。我有什麼好在意的？不過，我並沒有離開。不會的，我不會離開他。沒錯，在我們重修舊好之前，我都要很小心。他大部份的時間都住在湖邊的那些村落裡。他來到河岸時，偶爾會對我發怒，所以我最好小心點。這個人承受太多了，他討厭這鬼地方，但他離不開。之前，我有個機會哀求他，趁還有時間時，想辦法離開這裡，我願意跟他一起回去。他説好，可是之後依然繼續他進行又一趟的象牙狩獵，要不然就是消失幾個星期。跟他們那些人在一起，他就會忘了他自己。」

「哎，他瘋了！」我説。

P.53

庫爾茲

• 從那位俄國人的談話中，得知了庫爾茲的什麼事？和夥伴討論。

他聽了很不以為然，庫爾茲不可能發瘋，他是一個這麼健談又優秀的人。但顯然地，從那個俄國人所説的來看，庫爾茲對象牙永無止盡的胃口，導致他對象牙的獲取之道的看法，逐漸地改變了。

俄國人隨即説道，庫爾茲突然病得很重，他説：「聽説他只能無助地躺著，所以我來這裡碰碰運氣。他的狀況很不妙。」

庫爾茲在山坡上的屋子，破落的屋頂、長泥牆和三個不同大小的方形窗戶，看起來毫無生命的氣息。

我用望遠鏡再看了一次，這次卻看到了讓我震驚的景象。

建築物外面的圍牆柱子上，每根柱子頂端都有一個人頭。我知道這些人頭表

示庫爾茲已經失去自制力了。他會做任何他需要做的事，他的道德感和遠見已經喪失在荒野之中了。

P. 54

俄國人跟我說，他不敢把那些人頭拿下來。他不怕那些土著，除非有庫爾茲的命令，他們不敢妄動。庫爾茲的權力異常的大。土著就紮營在四周，酋長每天都來見他。他打算開始描述土著是怎麼接近庫爾茲的，但是被我制止。

「我一點都不想知道土著接近他時所使用的儀式。」我大吼著。

不知怎麼的，我覺得這些細節的描述，比圍牆柱子上乾掉的人頭，更令人難以接受。我對庫爾茲的態度，似乎讓那個俄國人感到吃驚。

P. 55

俄國人說：「我不懂。我已經盡最大的努力救他了。那些人頭和儀式，不關我的事，那些是造反者的人頭。這裡已經好幾個月都沒有任何的藥物，或是像樣的食物了。可恥的是，庫爾茲已經被放棄了。像他這樣的人，帶著這樣的理想……」

忽然間，庫爾茲的房子轉角出現一群人，他們抬著一個擔架，穿過高高的草地。剎時，一個大聲的尖叫聲，像尖銳的箭一樣，劃過天際。

P. 57

接著，像魔法一樣，人群魚貫而出，他們手上拿著矛，帶著弓和盾，用凶猛

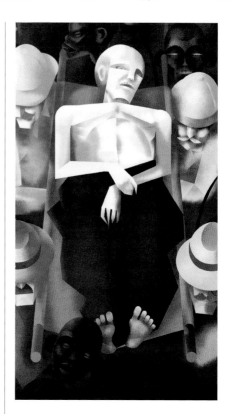

的神情狂暴地掃視周圍。他們湧入房子前方的空地，然後一切又寂靜下來了。

「現在，庫爾茲如果對他們講錯話，我們就全完了。」俄國人站在我旁邊觀察著說道。

那些抬著擔架的人，他們朝著我們所在的汽船走到一半時停住了，這時躺在擔架上的人坐了起來。

我說：「期待這個可以高談愛情的人，能夠找到一個好理由，來解救我們。」

透過望遠鏡，我看到庫爾茲威嚴地的舉著他纖細的手臂，口裡振振有詞的說著，雖然我們什麼都聽不見。

突然間，他往後倒下，抬擔架的人繼

續往前移動。同時間，我注意到人群退回森林裡，消失的速度就和出現一樣快。

有些總部來的人，拿著庫爾茲的槍，跟在擔架後走。經理走在擔架旁，和他說著話。

他們把他放在汽船上的一個小客艙裡，房間裡只夠容納一張床和兩張露營用的小板凳。我們把他的信帶來，床上擺滿了許多打開的信件和文件。

他拿起其中一封信，直視著我說：「我很高興。」

P. 58

顯然地，有人在信裡跟他提到了我。他看起來病得很重，連要小聲說一句話的力氣都沒有，但他嚴肅、低沉而富情感的聲音，打動了我！

預期

- 馬洛還沒「見到」庫爾斯，他就已經很瞭解他了。
- 在和某人未謀面之前，就已經很瞭解對方，你有過這樣的經驗嗎？
- 對方符合你的預期嗎？還是和你所想像的出入很大？

這時門口出現了經理，我往外走，對著俄國人和總部來的那些人走過去。我順著他們眼神的方向，看到了黑黑的人影在陰暗的森林邊緣移動著。

河邊站著兩名青銅色的人形，倚著高高的矛，戴著由斑點皮毛做的奇特頭飾，像要打戰似的，卻又安靜的站著。一位狂野又美麗的女人，沿著陽光照耀的河岸，從右邊到左邊地走著。

P. 60

她腳步緩慢，姿態很高，每走一步，身上的金屬飾品就發出叮噹

聲。她抬高頭，頭髮梳成頭盔的樣子，黃銅色的綁腿綁到膝蓋的位置，臂上有黃銅色的手套高至手肘，雙頰上有暗紅色的斑點。脖子上有許多由玻璃珠串起的項鍊，隨著步伐，晃動閃耀著。她看起來野蠻又華麗，緩慢持續的動作中，隱藏了些許危險的訊息。

她來到汽船邊，動也不動地看著我們。她臉上混雜了哀淒、害怕和痛苦。

周遭瀰漫著令人毛骨悚然的寂靜。

接著，她慢慢的轉身，沿著河岸走去。她在離開沒入森林之前，只回頭看了我們一眼。

「如果她想上船，我想我會開槍打她。過去這兩個星期以來，我每天都冒著生命的危險阻止她接近屋子。她進來過一次，大聲的和庫爾茲講了一個小時的話，並且不時地轉過來指著我。我聽不懂部落的方言。算我走運，庫爾茲那天病得太重，顧不了其他的了，不然我想我就有麻煩了。我不懂，這一切對我來說太沉重了。不過，現在都結束了。」俄國人說。

P. 61

這時，我聽到船艙裡傳來庫爾茲低沉的聲音。「救我！你是說救象牙吧！當我得救你時，不要跟我說救我這件事！你妨礙了我的計畫。病了？沒有你想得那麼嚴重。沒關係，我會繼續進行我的計畫，我會再回來！我會讓你看看可以做什麼。你和你小小的生意點子——你們都在妨礙我。我會再回來的。」

經理走出來，拉著我的手臂，我們走到船的一邊。

經理說：「他很沒水準，我們已經極盡所能的幫他了，不是嗎？但是不能忽略庫爾茲對公司過多功的事實。他在工作上太躁進了。謹慎、一步一步來，這是我的作風。我們要小心謹慎。這一區曾經和我們關係緊密。我不是說這裡沒有數量驚人的象牙，並且我們要全數保留。但是看看現在的情勢有多危險，而且為什麼會變成這樣？因為他的方法不好，他缺乏判斷力。我得向公司高層報告這件事。」

「但是，我覺得庫爾茲是個傑出的人。」我說。

「他以前是。」經理回答。他說完，便離開我身邊。

很明顯地，他認為我和庫爾茲一樣壞，也相信那些其實並不好的方法。我站錯邊了。

P. 62

俄國人拍拍我的肩膀。他說：「我覺得這些白人不喜歡我。」

「你說的對。如果這群土著裡有你的朋友，你大概最好還是先走吧。」我答道。

他回答：「有很多都是我的朋友。他們是一群單純的人，我對他們無所求。但是我也不希望這些白人發生什麼事，我擔心庫爾茲的名聲。我們都是船員，所以我做了什麼，我只告訴你一個人。」

一會兒後，我說：「沒事的，我不會說出去讓庫爾茲的名聲受影響。」

他低聲的跟我說，汽船的攻擊行動是庫爾茲下的指令。

他繼續說道：「他討厭撤離此地的計畫，他想要把你們嚇跑。我阻止不了他。哦，我上個月過得很淒慘啊！」

「謝啦，我會提高警覺。」我說。

「我有一艘獨木舟，還有三名土著在不遠處等著。我要走了。可以請你給我一些子彈嗎？還要一雙鞋子。」

我給了他一些子彈，還有一雙舊鞋子。

「啊，我再也遇不到這樣的人了。你應該聽過他朗誦詩吧，他跟我說，那是他自己做的詩。詩！喔，他真是讓我開了眼界。」

我說：「再見。」

我們握了手，然後他就消失在夜色中了。

第六章

P. 63

　　午夜時分，當我一醒來，我可以看到屋子旁的山丘上正燒著熊熊大火，而森林裡也有火光閃爍著，庫爾茲的仰慕者正在那裡等候的。我可以聽見緩慢的鼓聲和許多吟唱的聲音。我瞄了一下小船艙。燭光亮著，但庫爾茲並不在艙內。

　　起初我並不相信，因此應該是不可能的。我瞭解到，這表示我們可能隨時會被攻擊，但是我並沒有發出警報，也沒有告訴任何一個正在甲板上睡覺的公司仲介商。

　　不能背叛庫爾茲，已經變成我的工作了。我已經做了決定，選擇了與他同一陣線的噩夢。

　　我走下汽船，踏上河邊，看見高草的草地上有足跡。顯然地，庫爾茲已經偷偷溜走了。

　　最後我終於找到他了。他起身，長長的身子很蒼白，搖搖晃晃的。

　　「走開，去把自己藏起來。」他用低沉的嗓音說著。

P. 65

　　「你知道你在做什麼嗎？」我小聲地說。

　　「當然。」他提高音量回答。

　　「你會輸的，而且會輸得很徹底。」我說。

　　「我有個大計畫，我要做出偉大的事情，但是現在卻因為這個笨蛋經理……」他咕噥的說。

　　「不管發生什麼事，你在歐洲的成功是無庸置疑的。」我想用一些對他而言是很重要的事情來打動他。

　　我知道他的成就是前無古人後無來者的。庫爾茲是孤獨的，我看著他在欲望與希望中掙扎。我察覺到可怕的危險，因為他可以輕易地叫土著來把我們都殺了。我想要打破那個緊緊縛住著他的荒野詛咒。

　　信不信由你，他的思緒很清晰——專注，他的思緒全在他自己的身上，十分強烈可怕，但也很清晰。這是我唯一的機會：訴諸於他的理智。（另一個選擇，是當下殺了他，但是這不太好，因為之後會發出聲響。）

　　但他的靈魂已經瘋了。獨自一人在這荒野裡，就只能照看他的內心，天啊，我告訴你，他已經瘋了。現在也輪到我好好的來研究他的靈魂了。他自始至終都很有說服力，也很真誠。他自己也很掙扎。我看見了，也聽見了。我看到一個沒有束縛、沒有信仰、沒有畏懼，只有自己盲目掙扎著的靈魂，其中所隱藏著難以想像的祕密。

P. 66

　　最後，我拉了他一把，他纖細的手臂環繞著我的脖子，回到汽船上。

　　我們隔天中午離開。土著又從森林裡冒出來，占滿了山丘上那間屋子下面的地方。兩千隻眼睛盯著汽船看。三個全身塗滿亮紅色泥巴、頭上有角的人，在眾人前面上下走動，跺著腳，對著我們甩動黑色羽毛。他們大聲吼叫，眾人反覆吟唱。

　　庫爾茲坐在我的船長艙裡的沙發上看

著。忽然間，那個有著頭盔髮型的女人跑到岸邊。她伸出雙手，口中喊叫著，眾人繼續合聲怒吼著。

「你看懂這一切嗎？」我問。

他的眼神越過我，用熱烈渴望的雙眼，和混雜著渴望與仇恨的表情，繼續看著外面。

「我當然懂。」他緩慢地說，唇上帶著一抹意義深遠的微笑。

我拉了氣笛的繩子，因為我看到了總部的仲介商們拿出了槍。突然的尖銳笛聲，使得廣大人群中瀰漫著全然的恐懼。我一再地鳴笛，人們掙扎扭轉地逃走。那三個身上紅紅的人彷彿被殺了一樣，臉朝下的趴在河岸。只有那個狂野自傲的女人不為所動，在我們通過閃亮的河面後，她伸著手臂。

P. 67

棕色的潮水，從黑暗之心傾洩而出，帶領著我們往海洋而下，行進的速度是我們駛向上游的兩倍。而庫爾茲的生命也在快速的流逝中，從他的心，流往時間之海。經理很安靜，他覺得事情如他所願地落幕了。

庫爾茲說話了。那聲音！那聲音！低吟到最後。他的腦海裡，充滿了模糊的畫面，那是名與利的畫面。他提到了，「我的未婚妻，我的駐所，我的工作，我的理想。」

汽船如我所預期的故障了，我們要在小島旁等待修復。這次的延誤，動搖了庫爾茲的信心。

一天早晨，他給了我一包用鞋帶綁在一起的文件和一張照片。

他説：「幫我保管。我不在時，這個笨蛋（指經理）會偷看我的盒子。」

因為我要幫忙修理引擎，所以我沒有太多時間去理會庫爾茲。

一天晚上，我拿著蠟燭走進來，驚訝的聽到他説：「我躺在這等死。」

「胡説！」我回答道。

P. 68

他的臉色變了，我看見混雜著驕傲、力量、恐懼的表情，那個恐懼來自強烈的絕望。

在那當下，他又活了過來嗎？

他叫喊了兩次，那個叫喊，氣如游絲，喊著「恐懼！恐懼！」

第七章

P. 69

我把蠟燭吹熄，離開船艙。我走去和總部來的同事一起吃晚餐。突然，經理的兒子探出頭，在門邊説道：「庫爾茲先生，死了。」

除了我繼續吃著晚餐外，其他的人都衝過去看了。但是，我沒什麼食欲。那裡有一盞燈，但之外的地方是全然地黑暗。我沒再靠近那位引人注目的人。

隔天，仲介商們把他埋在泥濘的洞裡。那聲音消逝了，但是直到最後我還是不斷地做著那個惡夢，再次對庫爾茲展現我的忠誠。

命運，我的命運！他是個了不起的人。他有話要說。他看過太多了，他的眼界寬廣得足以容納整個宇宙，敏銳得足以看透在黑暗之中跳動的心。

他做出了總結，他評斷過了——「恐懼！」他的嘶吼是一種斷言，是一種道德上的勝利，勝利的代價是許多的挫敗、驚駭的恐懼和可怕的滿足感。但總歸還是一種勝利！這就是為什麼一直到最後我都對庫爾茲保持忠誠的原因。

P. 70

忠誠

• 你是個忠誠的人嗎？和夥伴分享。

在我經歷了這一切之後，再回到倫敦後，我發現平凡人們的日常生活很可笑。我留著庫爾茲給我的那一堆文件，不知道該如何處理。

有一個公司的人來找我，說他們擁有那些文件的所有權。我讓他看〈鎮壓野蠻習俗〉的報告，但是在瞄了一眼後，他說那不是他要的。在他離開後，我就沒再見過他。

兩天後，有一個自稱是庫爾茲的表哥的人出現，他告訴我，庫爾茲原本是一個優異的音樂家。我始終無法確定庫爾茲是做什麼的，是畫家？還是記者？而我們兩個人都認同他是個全才。我給那位老先生一些不重要的家族信件，他高興地離開了。

最後，來了一位記者，他想要知道他這位「親愛的同事」的事蹟。

他告訴我，他覺得庫爾茲並不是一位好作家。「但是，天啊！這男人真會講，他能讓群眾群起激憤。你看，他有信念，他可以讓他自己相信任何事情。他足以成為激進政治黨派的出色領導人。」

P. 71

「哪個黨派？」我問。

「任何黨派，他是個極端份子，不是嗎？」那人回說。

我認同他的說法。我給了他可以出版的文件，如果他覺得值得寫的話，隨後他就滿意地離開了。

庫爾茲

• 把庫爾茲可以做的各種事情，列成一張表。

最後，我帶著一小疊信件和女孩的肖畫像離開。我覺得畫中女孩的表情很美，所以我決定要把信件和像交給她。

我感覺庫爾茲所擁有的東西，都透過我的手傳出去了：他的靈魂、身體、駐所、象牙和工作。留下來的，只剩他的回憶與未婚妻了，所以我要去見她。

我一如往常走向眼前這個庫爾茲所待過的房子。擔架上他的身影，瘋狂仰慕的土著，森林的陰暗處，河流，如心臟跳動的規律鼓聲——那心，是勝利的黑暗之心。

P.73

回憶中他對我說過的那些話，也跟著我。我記得他的哀求、威脅、巨大的渴望、他的卑劣，以及他靈魂中的痛苦。當我按門鈴時，他似乎正往外盯著我看，一種既接受也憎恨這個世界的凝視。我似乎聽到他微弱的喊著：「恐懼！恐懼！」

我坐在偌大起居室裡，那裡有三面從地板延伸到天花板的長型落地窗。起居室裡有著又高又冷的大理石火爐，角落裡有一台大型鋼琴。高高的門開了又關上。我站了起來。

她一身黑衣，臉色蒼白地走過來。她在服喪中。

他已經過世一年多了，但是她看起來像是要永遠記著他，哀悼他的離開。她深深的注視著我，眼神中有著自信與信任。但是當我們握手時，我在她的臉上看到很強烈的孤獨感。對她而言，只有這一刻他是消逝的。

我們坐下來，我輕輕地將包裹放在小桌子上。

她把手放在上面，喃喃說道：「你很瞭解他。」

我說：「在那裡，人與人很快就變得親近了。我瞭解他，一如人們可以相互瞭解一樣。」

「而且你崇拜他，認識他而不崇拜他，是不可能的。」她說。

P.74

「他是個了不起的人，不可能不……」我回答說。

「愛他。」她很快地接了話，讓我啞口無言。「真的！但是沒有人像我這麼瞭解他，我是最懂他的人。」

屋內愈來愈暗，但是她的額頭又光滑又潔白。她因為信仰與愛的內在光芒，而顯得容光煥發。

她繼續說：「你是他的朋友，如果他給了你這個，又叫你來找我，你們一定是朋友。我覺得我可以跟你說。喔，我一定要告訴你。你是聽到他的遺言的人，我要你知道我配得上他。」

我聽著。天色愈來愈暗。她就像口渴的人飢渴地喝著水一樣，滔滔不絕得講著。

「聽過他說話的人，誰不會成為他的朋友呢？」她繼續說著：「他可以讓所有認識的人，表現出最好的自己，這是他的天賦。你聽過他說話，你是知道的。」

我說：「對，我知道。」

「對我、對我們、對這個世界來說，這是多大的損失啊。」我可以看到她眼眶中含著滿滿的淚水，她繼續說著：「我曾經非常快樂、非常幸運，也非常自豪，太幸運了。我有一小段時間，太幸福了。但是現在的我並不快樂，這輩子都不會了。他的承諾、偉大、慷慨的心胸、尊貴的心靈，什麼都沒有留下，除了回憶，什麼都沒有。而你和我……」

「我們會永遠記著他的。」我很快地接話。

崇拜

• 你想，為什麼會有這麼多不同的
  人，出於各種不同的理由，而喜
  愛、崇拜庫爾茲？

「他所說的話將流傳下來，還有他的榜樣。人們尊敬他，他所做的一切，都體現著他的良善。我無法相信我已經再也見不到他了，再也沒有人會見到他了，永遠都不會了。」她說。

她伸出手臂，像是有人要離開了一樣。再也看不到他！但當然我清楚地看到他。在我有生之年，我都會看到他能言善語的魅影。

「你一直陪伴他，直到最後嗎？」

我顫抖著說：「一直到最後，我聽見他最後說的那些話⋯⋯」我害怕的停了下來。

「再說一次那些話，我需要可以讓我繼續活下去的東西。」她心碎的呢喃著。

現在屋內愈來愈黑了，而那黑暗似乎正在重複著：「恐懼！恐懼！」

「讓我帶著他最後所說的話，活下去。」她堅持地說：「難道你不懂我愛他嗎？我愛他！」

我專注地緩慢道出，「他最後說出的話是——你的名字。」

我聽到短促的嘆息聲，接著一聲響亮可怕的哭喊聲，聲音中帶著難以置信的勝利和極度的痛苦。

「我就知道，我很確定！」她說。

她知道，她確定。她把臉埋在手裡啜泣著。

庫爾茲總是說他要正義。但是我沒辦法，沒辦法告訴她真相。這一切都太黑暗、太黑暗，整個都太黑暗了。

馬洛以這些話來結束他的故事。

他一個人安靜的坐在一旁，一時之間，聶力號上沒有人有動靜。天空是黑的，河流也是黑的，像是要將我們帶往無邊無際的黑暗之心一樣。

Before Reading

1
a) wilderness
b) desolate
c) natives
d) canoe
e) journey
f) steamboat

3
* Taken to Africa:
  beads/cotton/alcohol
* Brought back from Africa:
  ivory/rubber/gold

4 Slavery.
5 a
6 a) 1 b) 3 c) 3 d) 1
7 1. Outer Station
    2. Central Station
    3. Inner Station

8 a) 2 b) 1 c) 3
9 A job with a lot of responsibilities, e.g.
    a managing director, an important
    businessman

10
a) imagine
b) lone
c) headquarters
d) colleagues
e) canoe
f) natives
g) desolate
h) wilderness

11 In Exercise 8 all comments are positive
    and describe a very successful person.
    Marlow's description is that of an
    isolated man who prefers life with
    the natives to life with his business
    colleagues.

* To Africa, up the Congo River.
* Belgian.

* Ivory. Out of Africa and into Europe.

Because he is a first-class agent and a
remarkable person.

They change according to their position
along the Congo River.

* Manager, three white agents, Marlow
  and twenty cannibals. To the inner
  station.

After Reading

Page 79

4 a) F b) T c) T d) F e) T f) F g) T h) F
  a) He is on a boat (the Nellie) on the river Thames.
  d) He is in Africa to bring back ivory.
  f) Everyone admired him, especially the natives.
  h) No, Kurtz dies in Africa before leaving.

5
a) broke down
b) admired
c) ill
d) journalist
e) papers
f) girlfriend

Pages 80-81

6 a) 3 b) 4 c) 2 d) 1

7
d) It's the beginning of the story. Marlow is on his boat on the Thames, waiting to leave, and he begins to tell his story.
c) Marlow is beginning his journey up the Congo River in Africa, going deep into the jungle.
a) Kurtz is being carried on a stretcher towards Marlow's boat. The natives don't want him to leave.
b) At the end of the story Marlow is visiting Kurtz's girlfriend in England and giving her the papers Kurtz gave him.

8
a) Kurtz
b) the accountant
c) Kurtz's girlfriend
d) Marlow

9
a) Kurtz said these words just before he died to no-one in particular.
b) The accountant is speaking to Marlow who has recently arrived in Africa.
c) Kurtz's girlfriend is speaking to Marlow at the end of the story. She is very sad.
d) Marlow was speaking to the company manager. He is defending Kurtz.

Pages 82-83

10
a) adventure, Africa
b) dark
c) trading, sail
d) sent
e) natives
f) loyal
g) mystery
h) focus
i) respected
j) tribe

12 Conrad, like Marlow, also went to Africa up the Congo River in 1890. He also became very ill. There is a strong autobiographical influence on the story.

Pages 84-85

13 a) 2 b) 3 c) 1

14 View of Africa – A mysterious place (p. 23) full of beauty and also danger (p.p. 35–36).
View of the colonizer – Generally cruel people (p. 24). Only interested in the ivory. (p.p. 24–25)

15 Kurtz's words could refer to several things: colonization in general, the exploitation of the natives, man's greed and cruelty or Africa itself.

16
a) Marlow goes from England to Belgium, back to England and then sails to Africa. He goes up the Congo River to the Inner Station.
b) He saw how the colonizers treated the natives and how Kurtz had tried to change this. He respected Kurtz, who lived with the natives and lost any respect for the white people in Africa.
c) Kurtz learnt to respect the natives more than his colleagues and preferred to live with them. He was living like an African native in a tribe when Marlow met him.

17 c) One of the friends on the *Nellie* and Marlow.

18 both a) and c) are possible

Pages 86-87

19
a) dark
b) dark
c) dark
d) darkness
e) darkness
f) darkness

20 b + e

21
a) power
b) escalator
c) nuclear energy
d) interconnection
e) the weather
f) turn on/off

22
a) anchored
b) current
c) bank
d) up river
e) down river

Test

Pages 88-89

1 a) 1   b) 2   c) 1   d) 2

2 a) 3   b) 3   c) 4   d) 1   e) 1
   f) 4   g) 4   h) 1   i) 3   j) 1

Project Work

Page 92

1
a) Fiji, Malaysia, Canada, Zimbabwe, Ireland, Tanzania, Antigua and Barbuda, Australia, Bahamas, Bangladesh, Barbados, Belize, Botswana, Brunei, Cameroon, Cyprus, Dominica, Gambia, Ghana, Grenada, Guyana, India, Jamaica, Kenya, Kiribati, Lesotho, Malawi, Maldives, Malta, Mauritius, Mozambique, Namibia, Nauru, New Zealand, Nigeria, Pakistan, Papua New Guinea, Rwanda, Saint Kitts and Nevis, Saint Lucia, Saint Vincent and the Grenadines, Samoa, Seychelles, Sierra Leone, Singapore, Solomon Islands, South Africa, Sri Lanka, Swaziland, Tonga, Trinidad and Tobago, Tuvalu, Uganda, Vanuatu and Zambia.

b) Officially it ended with the independence of Burma in 1948 although it began its gradual decline before and after the Second World War as, one by one, countries gained their independence.

c) Queen Victoria (1837-1901) reigned when the Empire was at its strongest.

國家圖書館出版品預行編目資料

黑暗之心 / Joseph Conrad 著；David A.
Hill改寫；林育珊 譯. 一初版. 一[臺北市]：
寂天文化, 2016.2 面；公分. 中英對照

ISBN 978-986-318-425-6 (平裝附光碟片)
　　1. 英語　　2. 讀本

805.18　　　　　　　　　　104028915

原著 _ Joseph Conrad

改寫 _ David A. Hill

譯者 _ 林育珊

校對 _ 陳慧莉

製程管理 _ 洪巧玲

出版者 _ 寂天文化事業股份有限公司

電話 _ +886-2-2365-9739

傳真 _ +886-2-2365-9835

網址 _ www.icosmos.com.tw

讀者服務 _ onlineservice@icosmos.com.tw

出版日期 _ 2016年2月 初版一刷（250101）

郵撥帳號 _ 1998620-0 寂天文化事業股份有限公司